MR. BADGER AND MRS. FOX #3

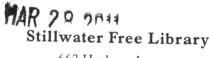

Brigitte **LUCIANI** & Eve **THARLET**

Graphic Universe™ • Minneapolis • New York • London

For Christian, Brigitte, Marguerite, and Edmond
for the escape they gave me . . .
—E.T.

Story by Brigitte Luciani
Art by Eve Tharlet
Translation by Edward Gauvin

First American edition published in 2011 by Graphic Universe™.
Published by arrangement with MEDIATOON LICENSING – France.

Monsieur Blaireau et Madame Renarde
3/Quelle équipe!
© DARGAUD 2009 – Tharlet & Luciani
www.dargaud.com

Graphic Universe™
A division of Lerner Publishing Group, Inc.
241 First Avenue North
Minneapolis, MN 55401 U.S.A.

Website address: www.lernerbooks.com

Library of Congress Cataloging-in-Publication Data available.

ISBN: 978-0-7613-5627-1

Manufactured in the United States of America
1 – DP – 12/31/10

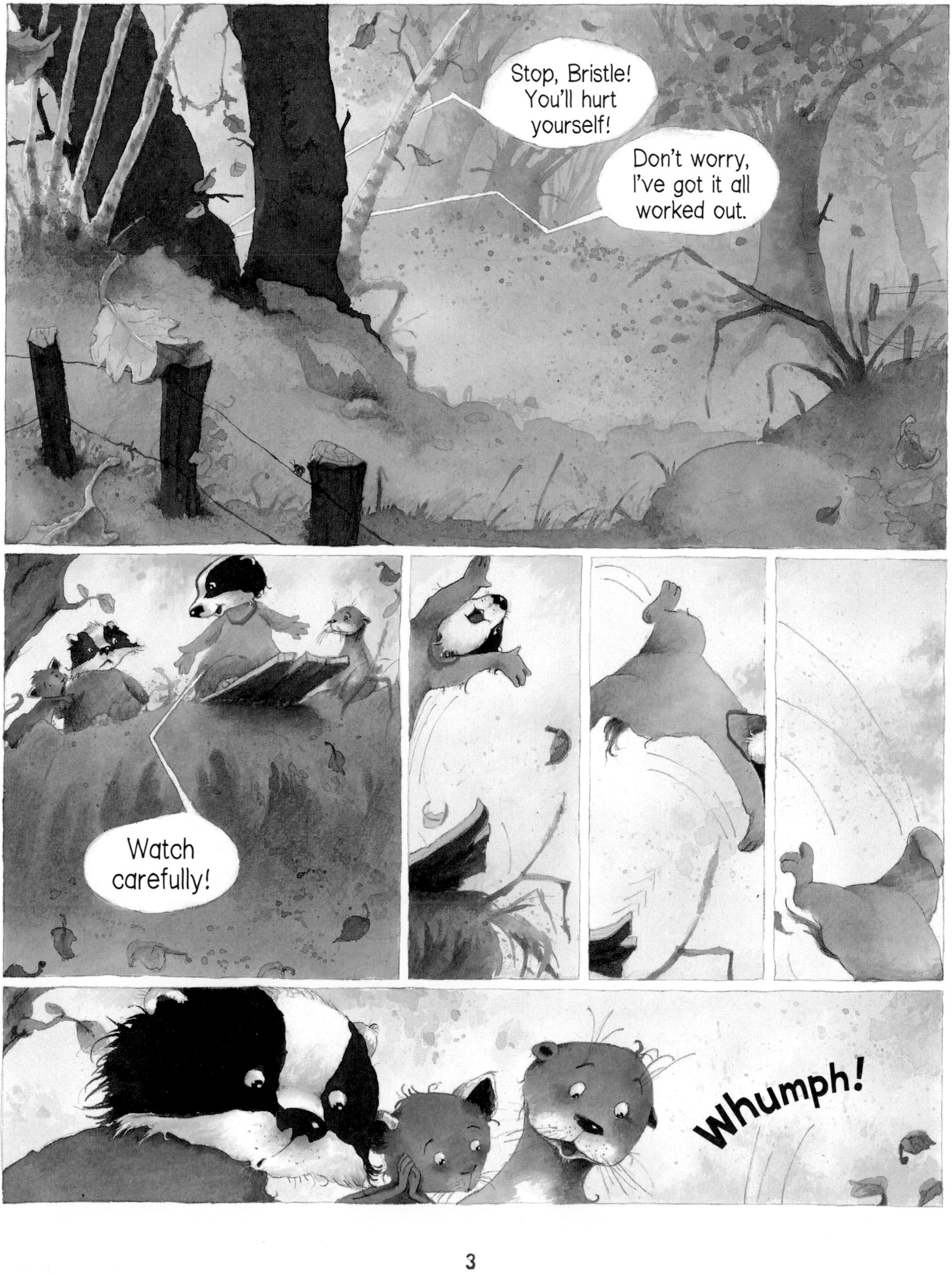
Stop, Bristle! You'll hurt yourself!
Don't worry, I've got it all worked out.
Watch carefully!
Whumph!

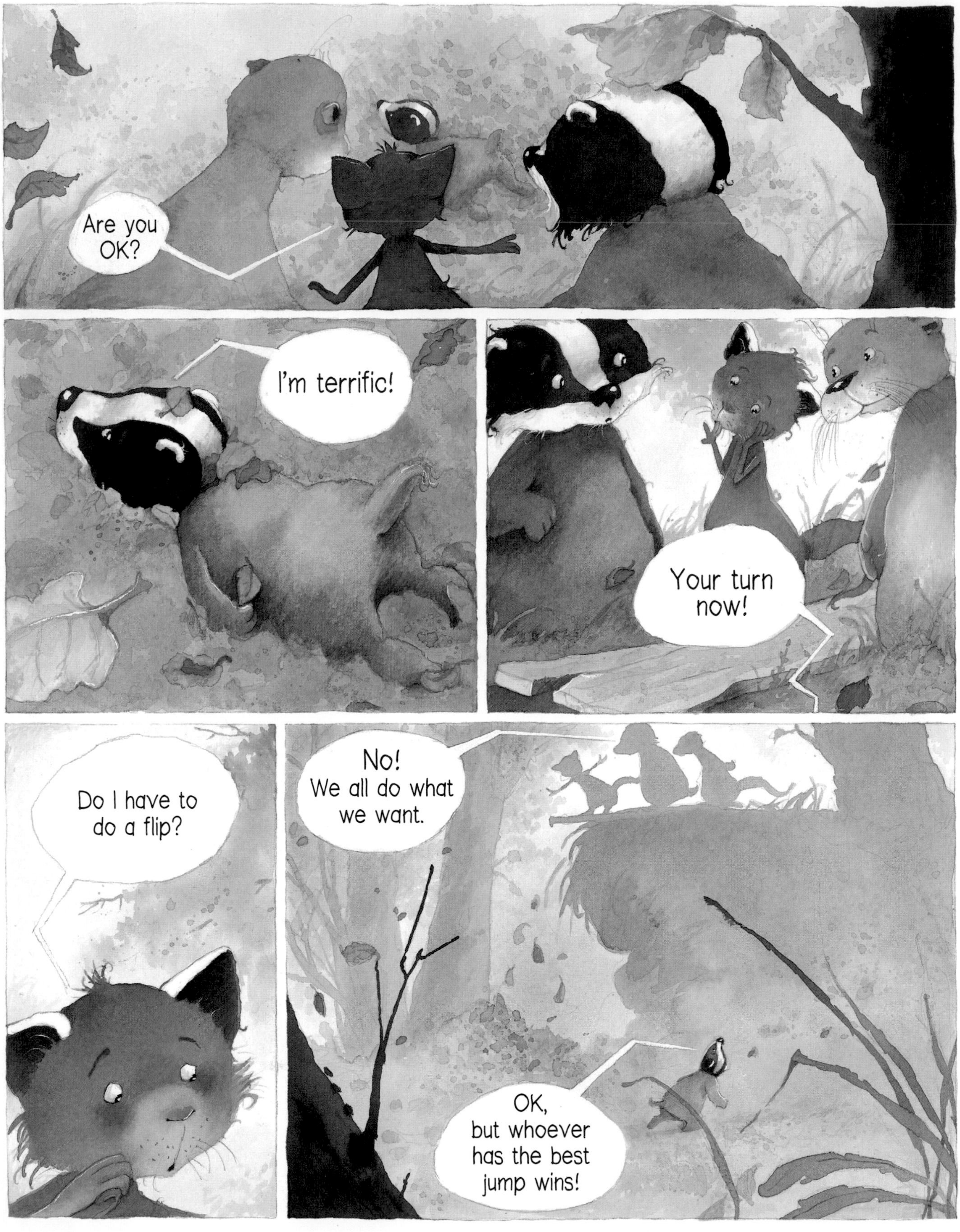

Are you OK?
I'm terrific!
Your turn now!
Do I have to do a flip?
No! We all do what we want.
OK, but whoever has the best jump wins!

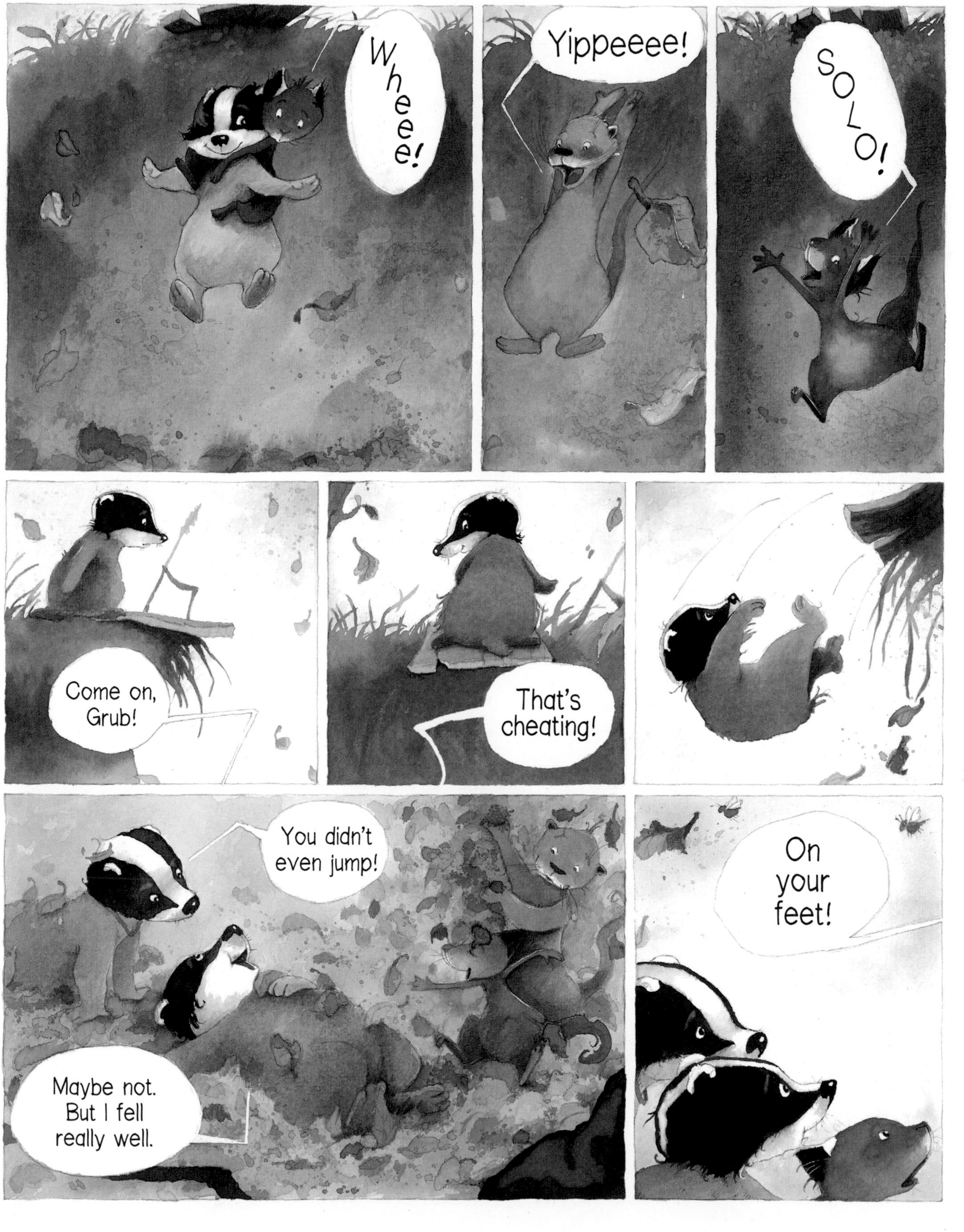
Wheee!
Yippeeee!
SOLO!
Come on, Grub!
That's cheating!
You didn't even jump!
Maybe not. But I fell really well.
On your feet!

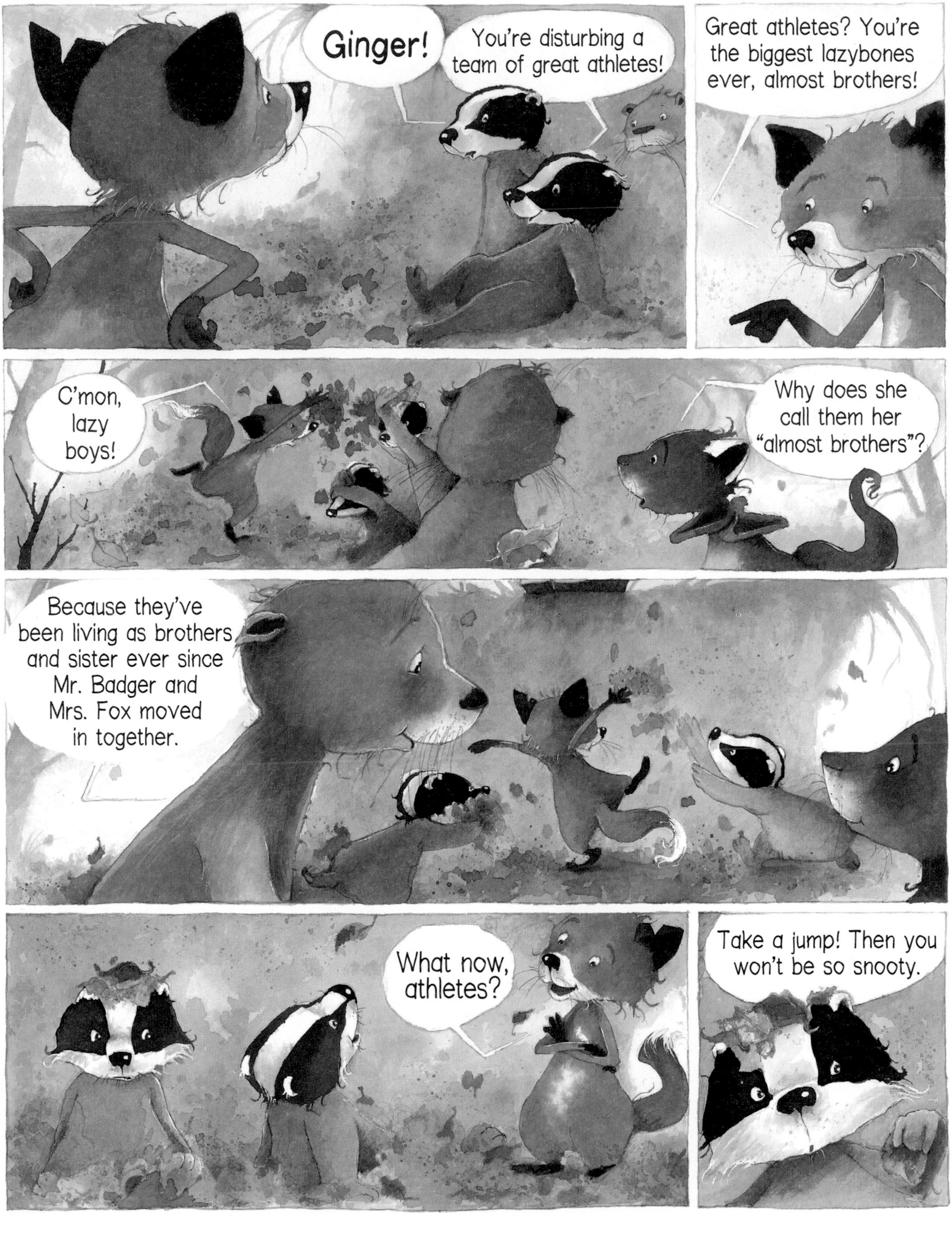
Ginger!
You're disturbing a team of great athletes!
Great athletes? You're the biggest lazybones ever, almost brothers!
C'mon, lazy boys!
Why does she call them her "almost brothers"?
Because they've been living as brothers and sister ever since Mr. Badger and Mrs. Fox moved in together.
What now, athletes?
Take a jump! Then you won't be so snooty.

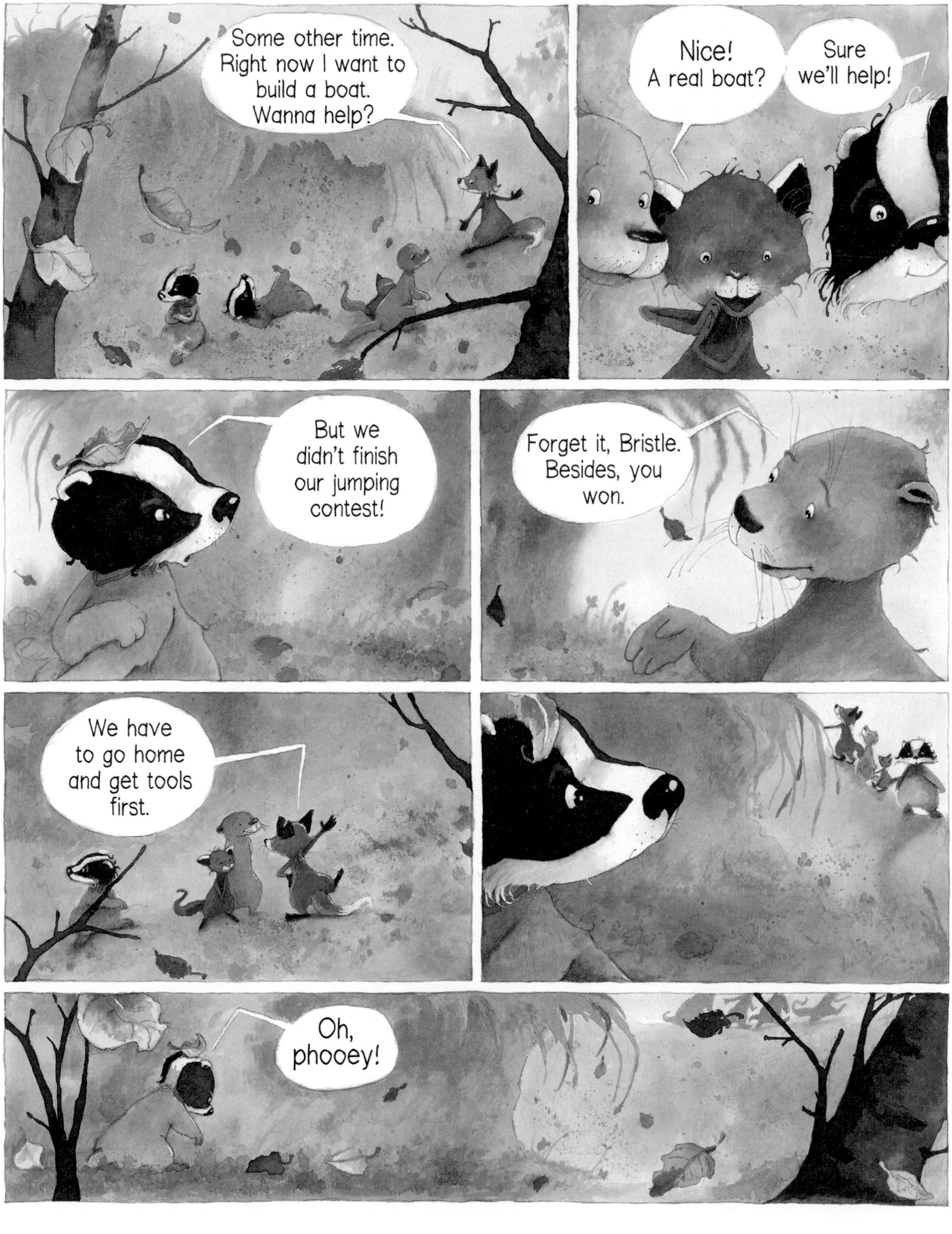

Some other time. Right now I want to build a boat. Wanna help?
Nice! A real boat?
Sure we'll help!
But we didn't finish our jumping contest!
Forget it, Bristle. Besides, you won.
We have to go home and get tools first.
Oh, phooey!

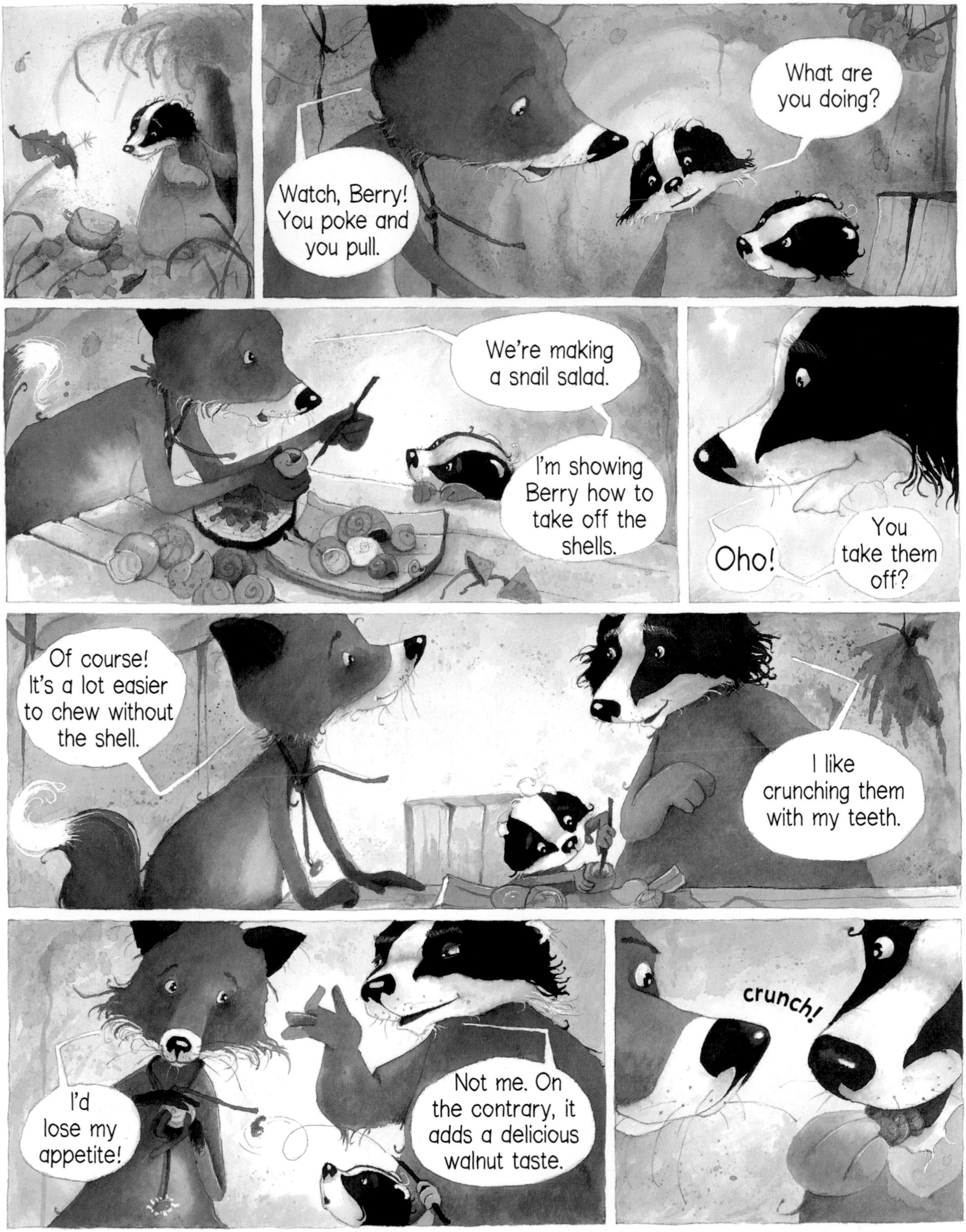

Watch, Berry! You poke and you pull.
What are you doing?
We're making a snail salad.
I'm showing Berry how to take off the shells.
Oho!
You take them off?
Of course! It's a lot easier to chew without the shell.
I like crunching them with my teeth.
I'd lose my appetite!
Not me. On the contrary, it adds a delicious walnut taste.
crunch!

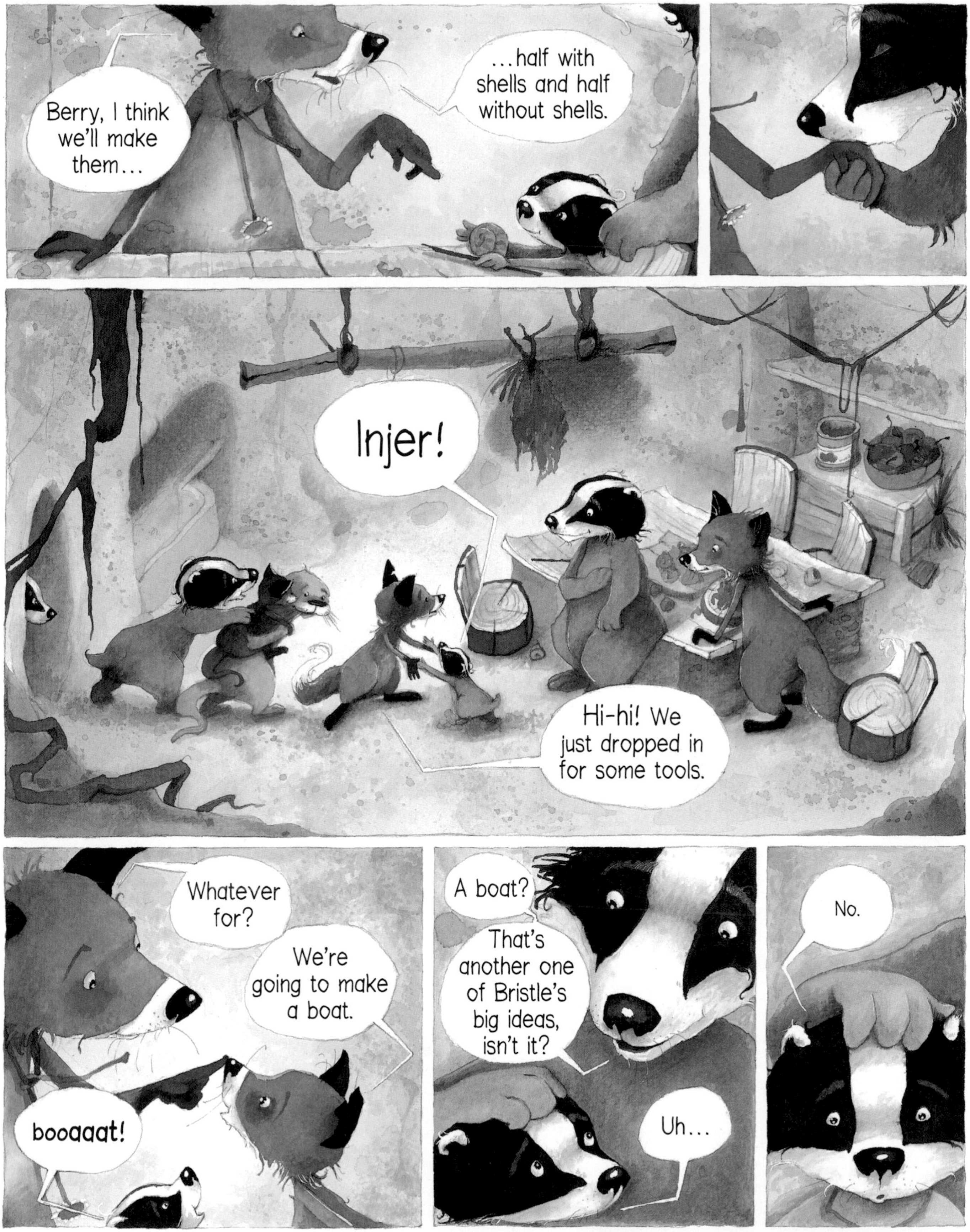
Berry, I think we'll make them...
...half with shells and half without shells.
Injer!
Hi-hi! We just dropped in for some tools.
Whatever for?
We're going to make a boat.
booaaat!
A boat?
That's another one of Bristle's big ideas, isn't it?
Uh...
No.

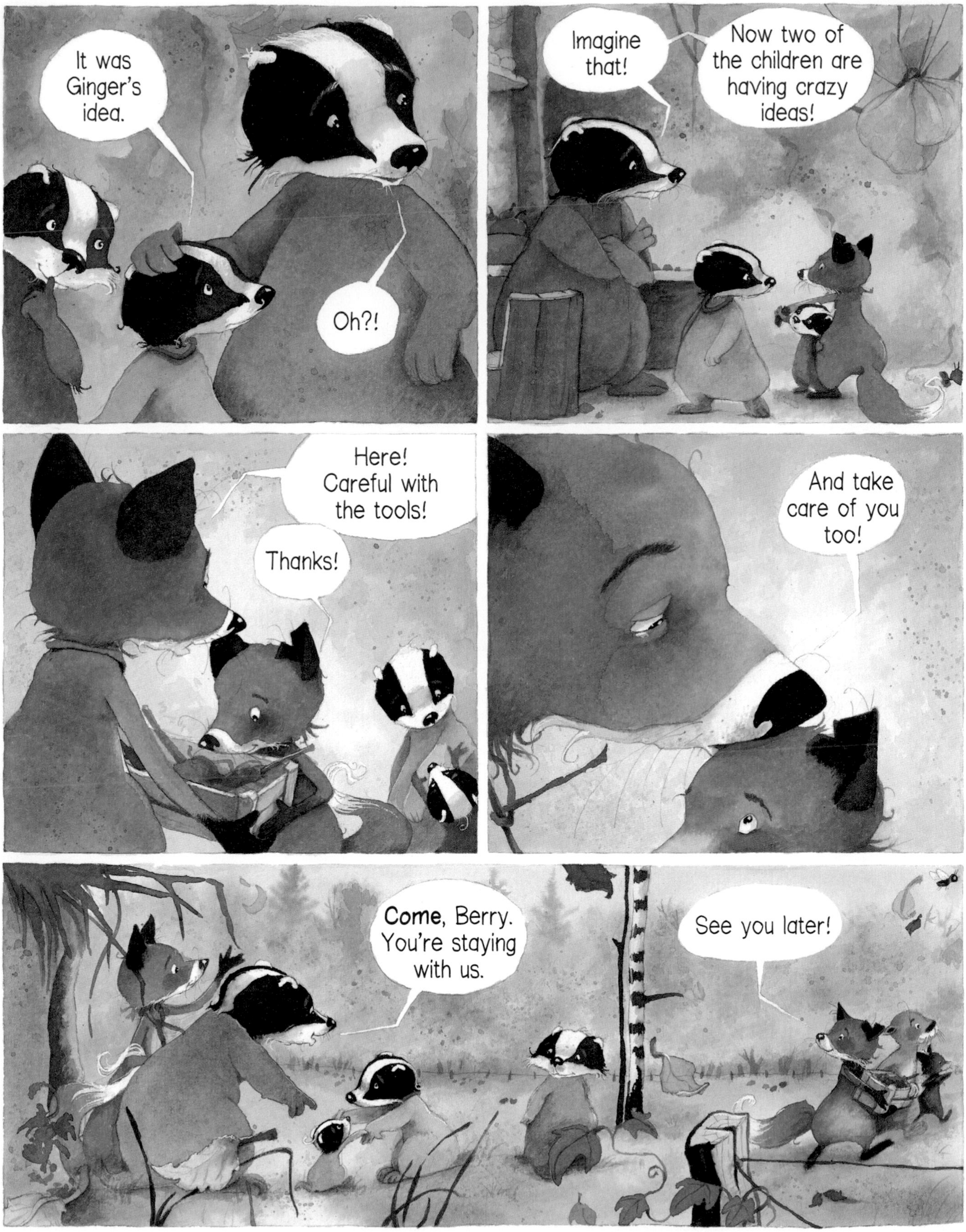
It was Ginger's idea.
Oh?!
Imagine that!
Now two of the children are having crazy ideas!
Here! Careful with the tools!
Thanks!
And take care of you too!
Come, Berry. You're staying with us.
See you later!

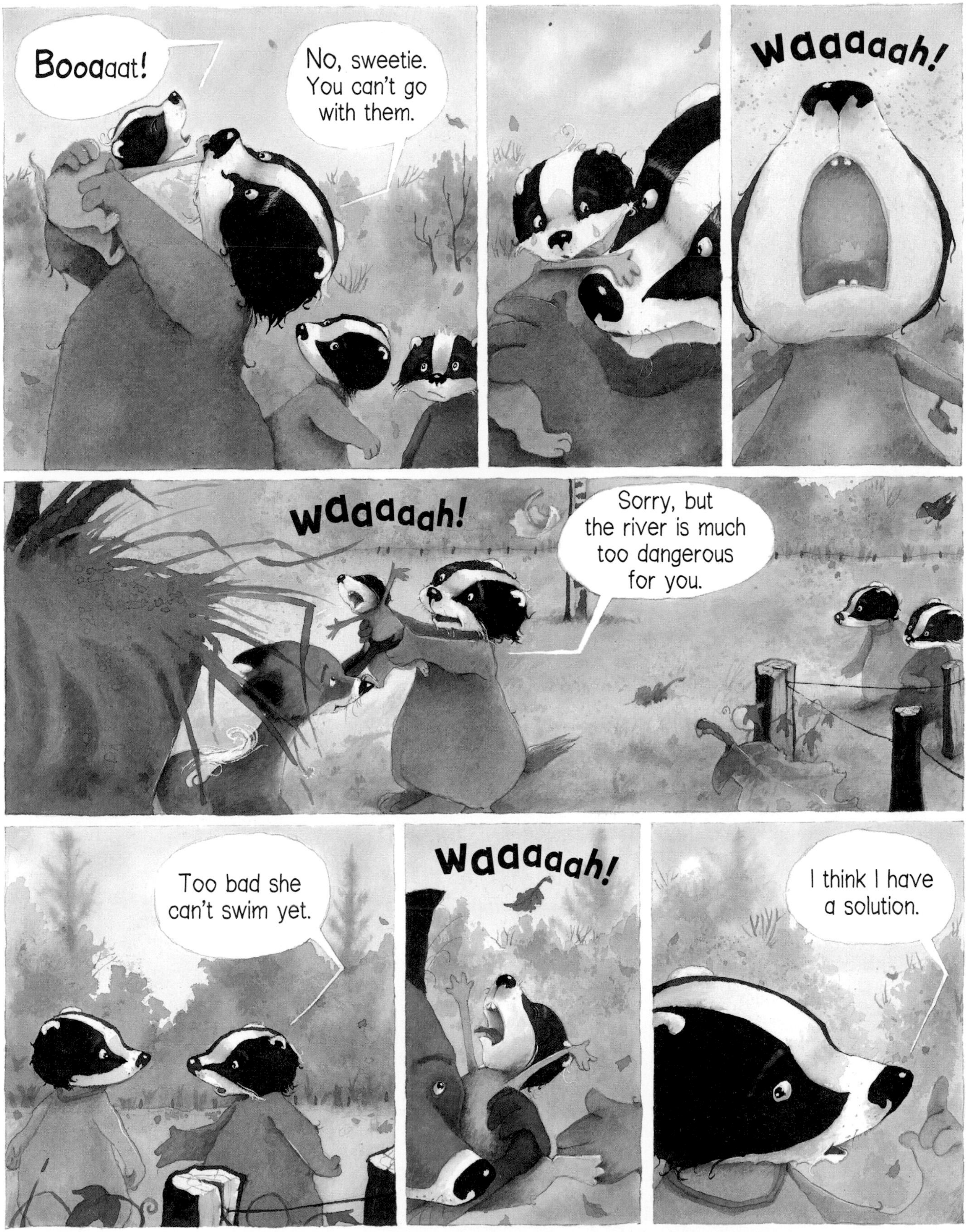
Booaaat!
No, sweetie. You can't go with them.
Waaaaah!
Waaaaah!
Sorry, but the river is much too dangerous for you.
Too bad she can't swim yet.
Waaaah!
I think I have a solution.

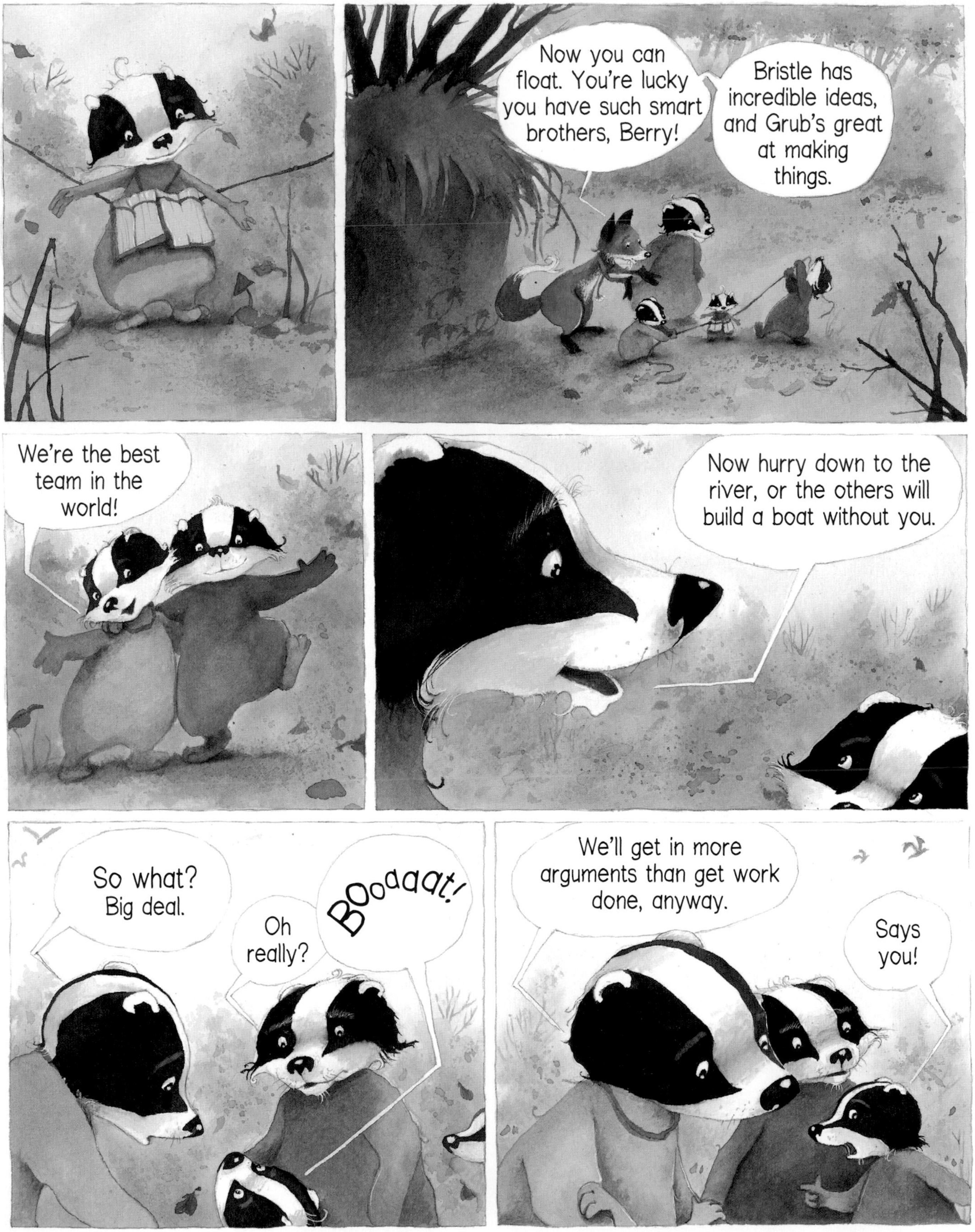
Now you can float. You're lucky you have such smart brothers, Berry!
Bristle has incredible ideas, and Grub's great at making things.
We're the best team in the world!
Now hurry down to the river, or the others will build a boat without you.
So what? Big deal.
Oh really?
BOoaaat!
We'll get in more arguments than get work done, anyway.
Says you!

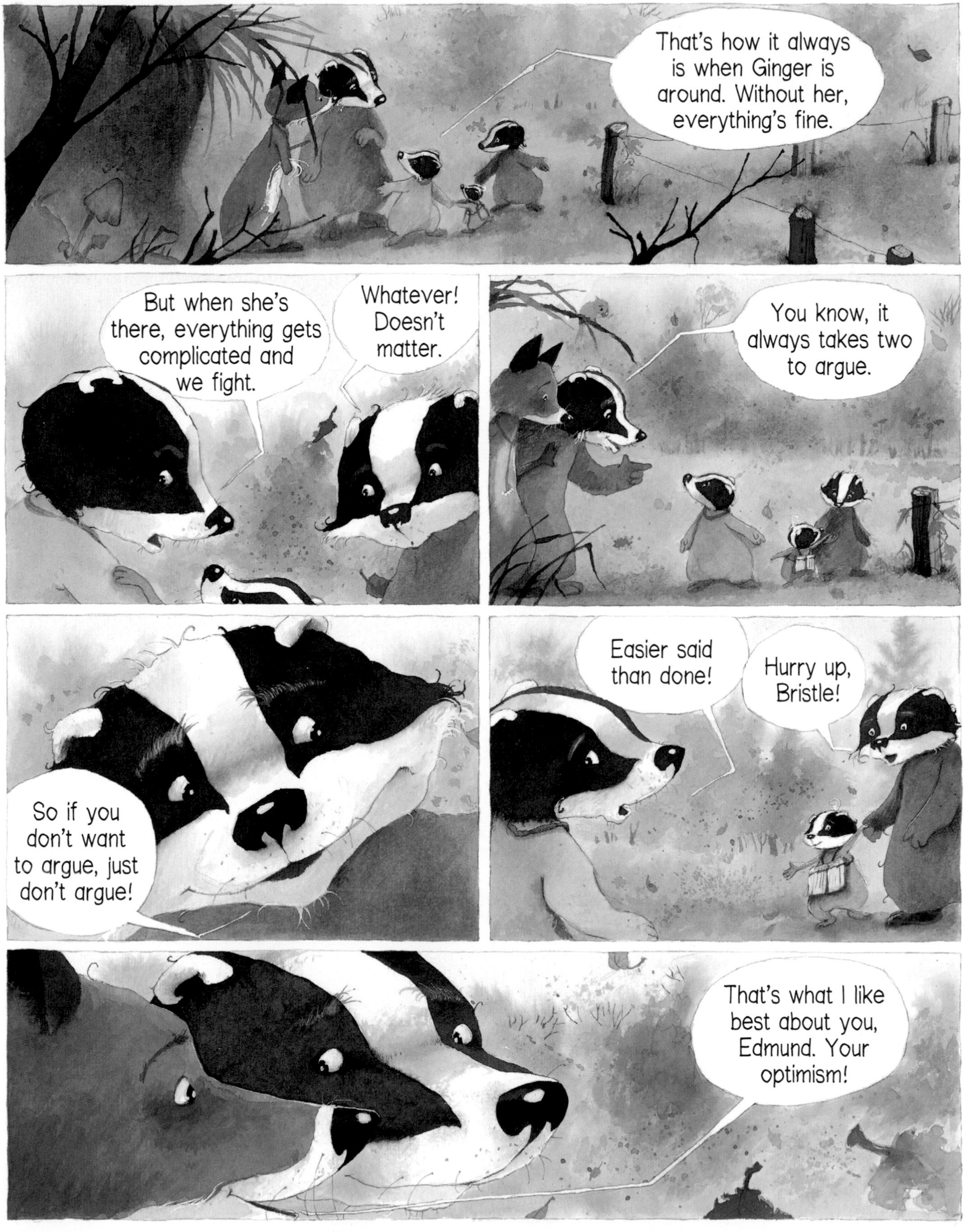
That's how it always is when Ginger is around. Without her, everything's fine.
But when she's there, everything gets complicated and we fight.
Whatever! Doesn't matter.
You know, it always takes two to argue.
So if you don't want to argue, just don't argue!
Easier said than done!
Hurry up, Bristle!
That's what I like best about you, Edmund. Your optimism!

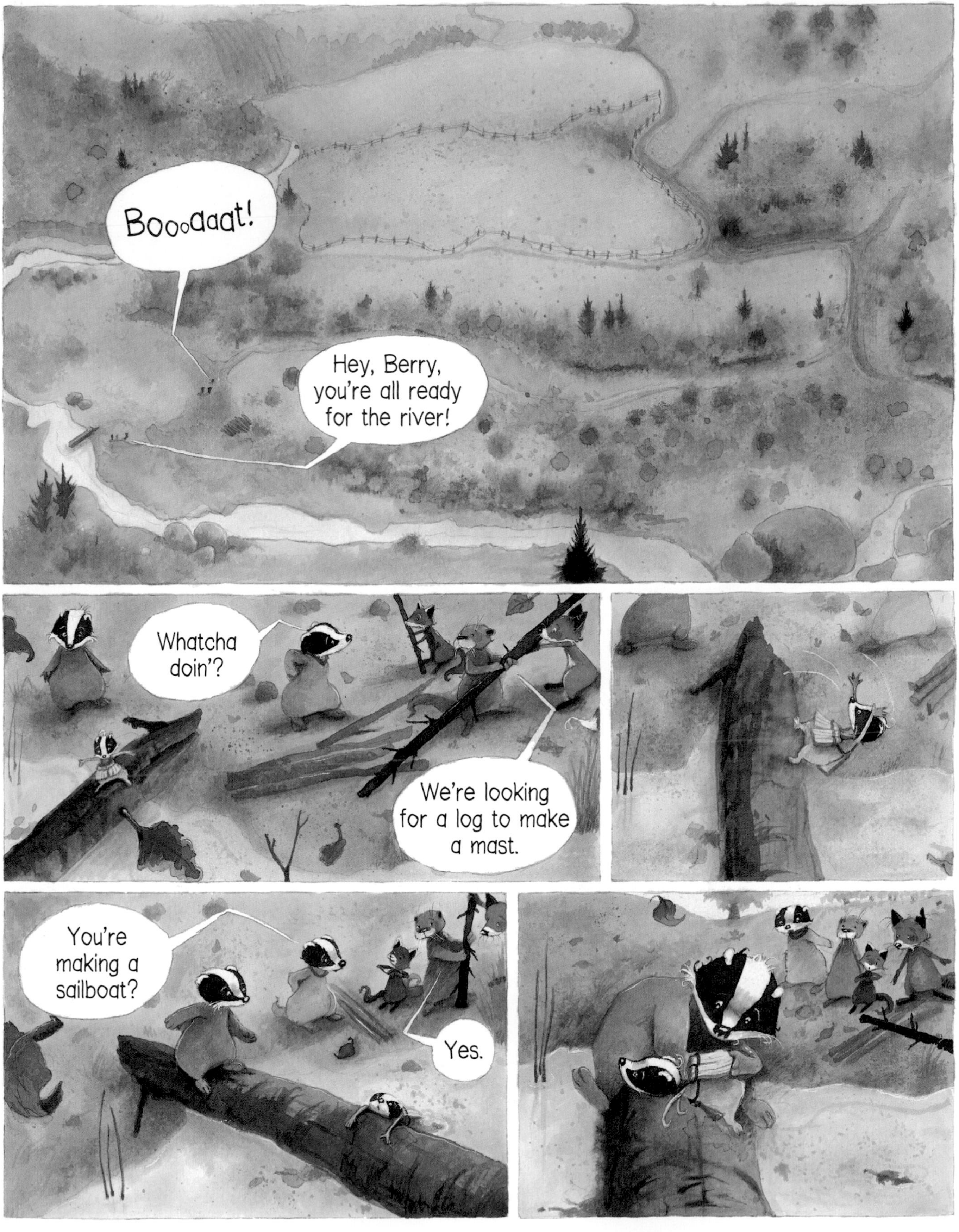
Booooaaat!
Hey, Berry, you're all ready for the river!
Whatcha doin'?
We're looking for a log to make a mast.
You're making a sailboat?
Yes.

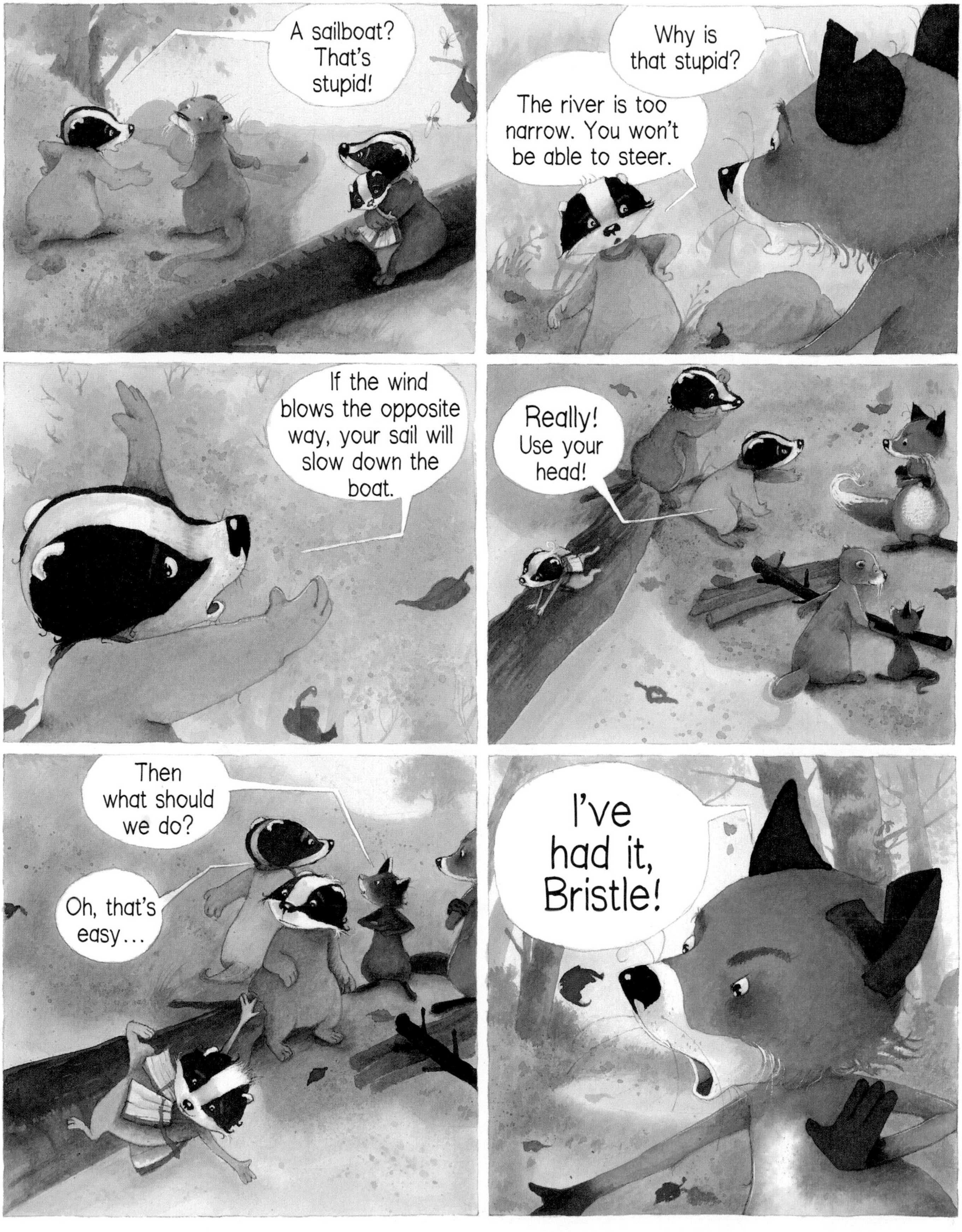
A sailboat? That's stupid!
Why is that stupid?
The river is too narrow. You won't be able to steer.
If the wind blows the opposite way, your sail will slow down the boat.
Really! Use your head!
Then what should we do?
Oh, that's easy...
I've had it, Bristle!

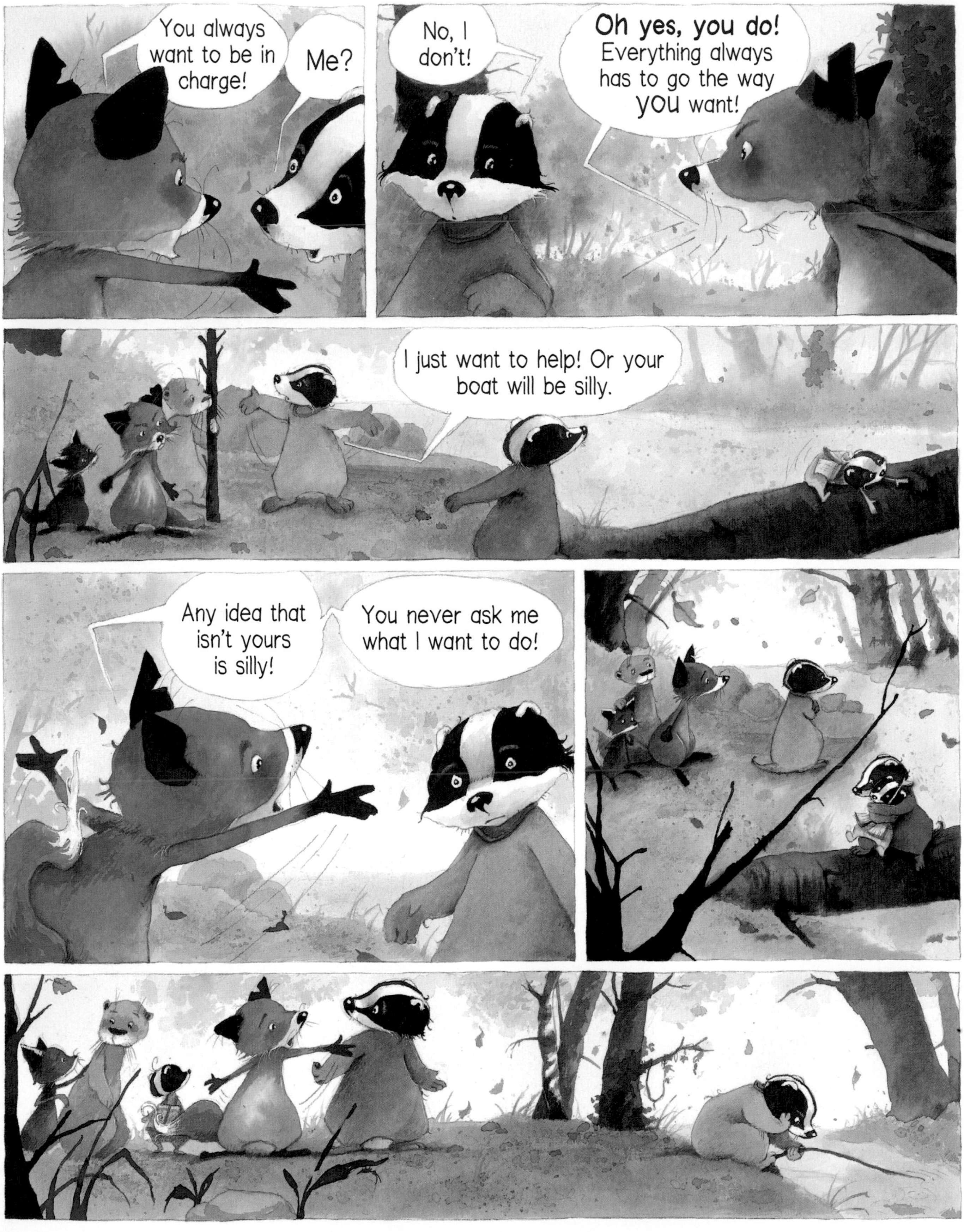
You always want to be in charge!
Me?
No, I don't!
Oh yes, you do! Everything always has to go the way YOU want!
I just want to help! Or your boat will be silly.
Any idea that isn't yours is silly!
You never ask me what I want to do!

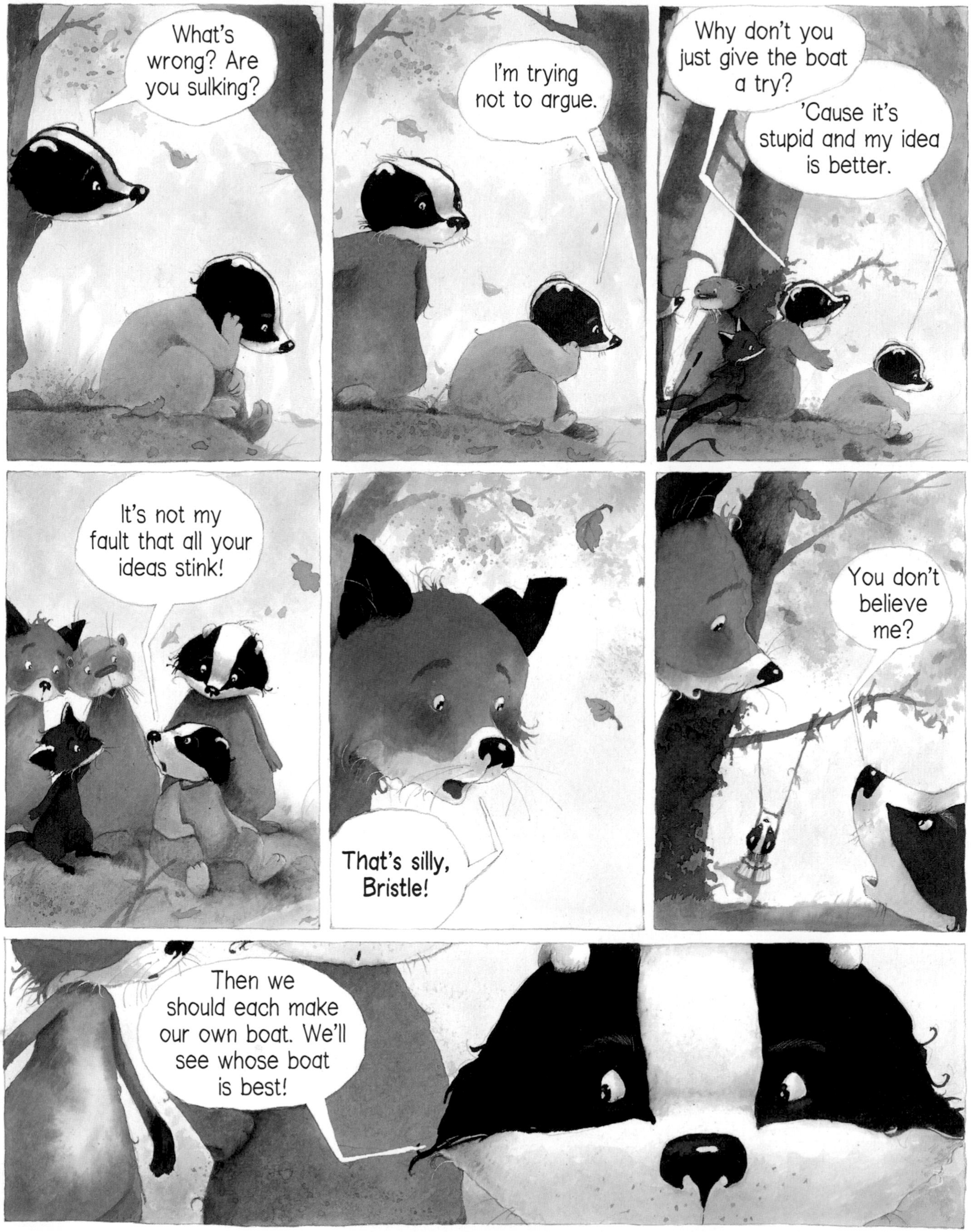
What's wrong? Are you sulking?
I'm trying not to argue.
Why don't you just give the boat a try?
'Cause it's stupid and my idea is better.
It's not my fault that all your ideas stink!
That's silly, Bristle!
You don't believe me?
Then we should each make our own boat. We'll see whose boat is best!

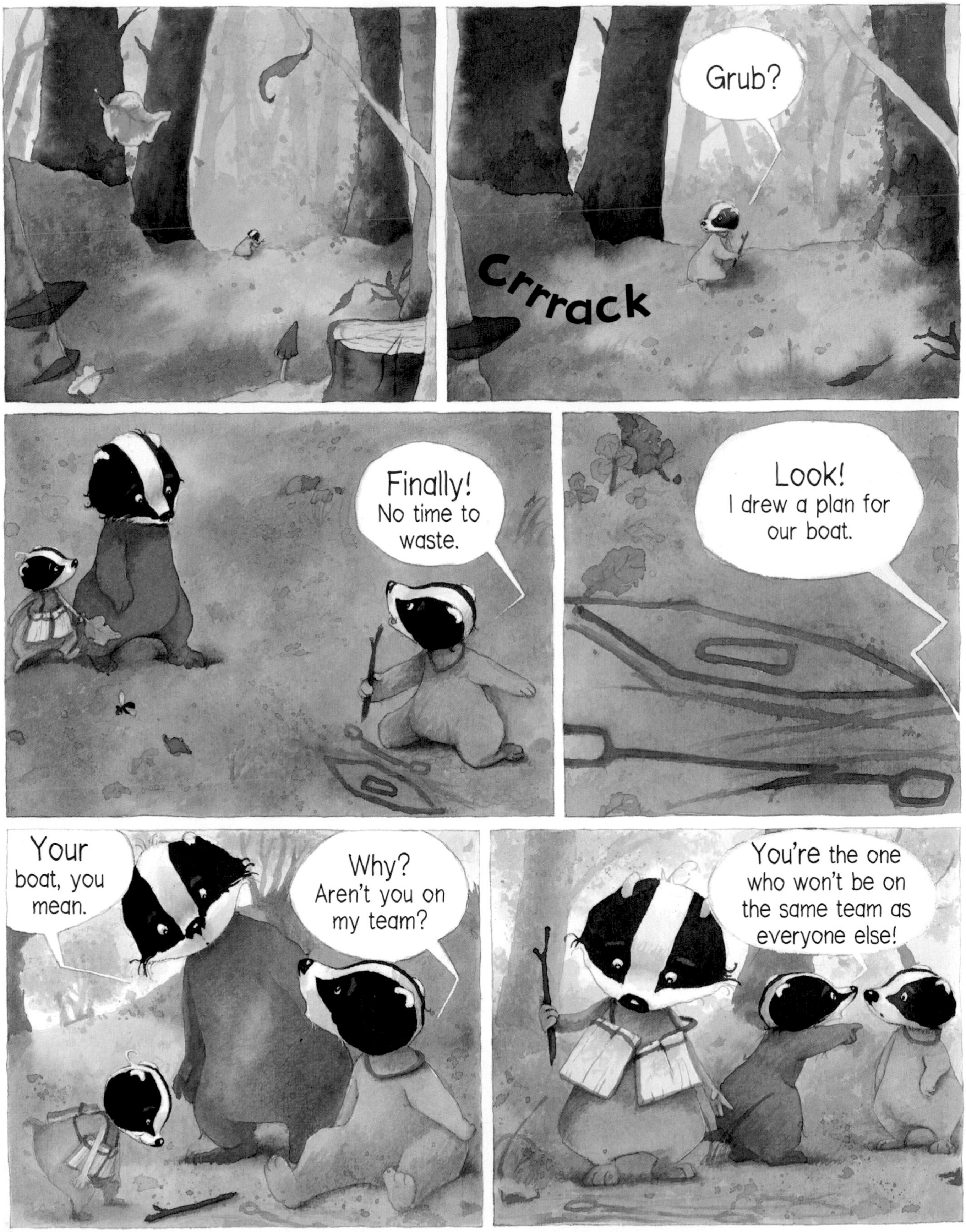
Grub?
Crrrack
Finally! No time to waste.
Look! I drew a plan for our boat.
Your boat, you mean.
Why? Aren't you on my team?
You're the one who won't be on the same team as everyone else!

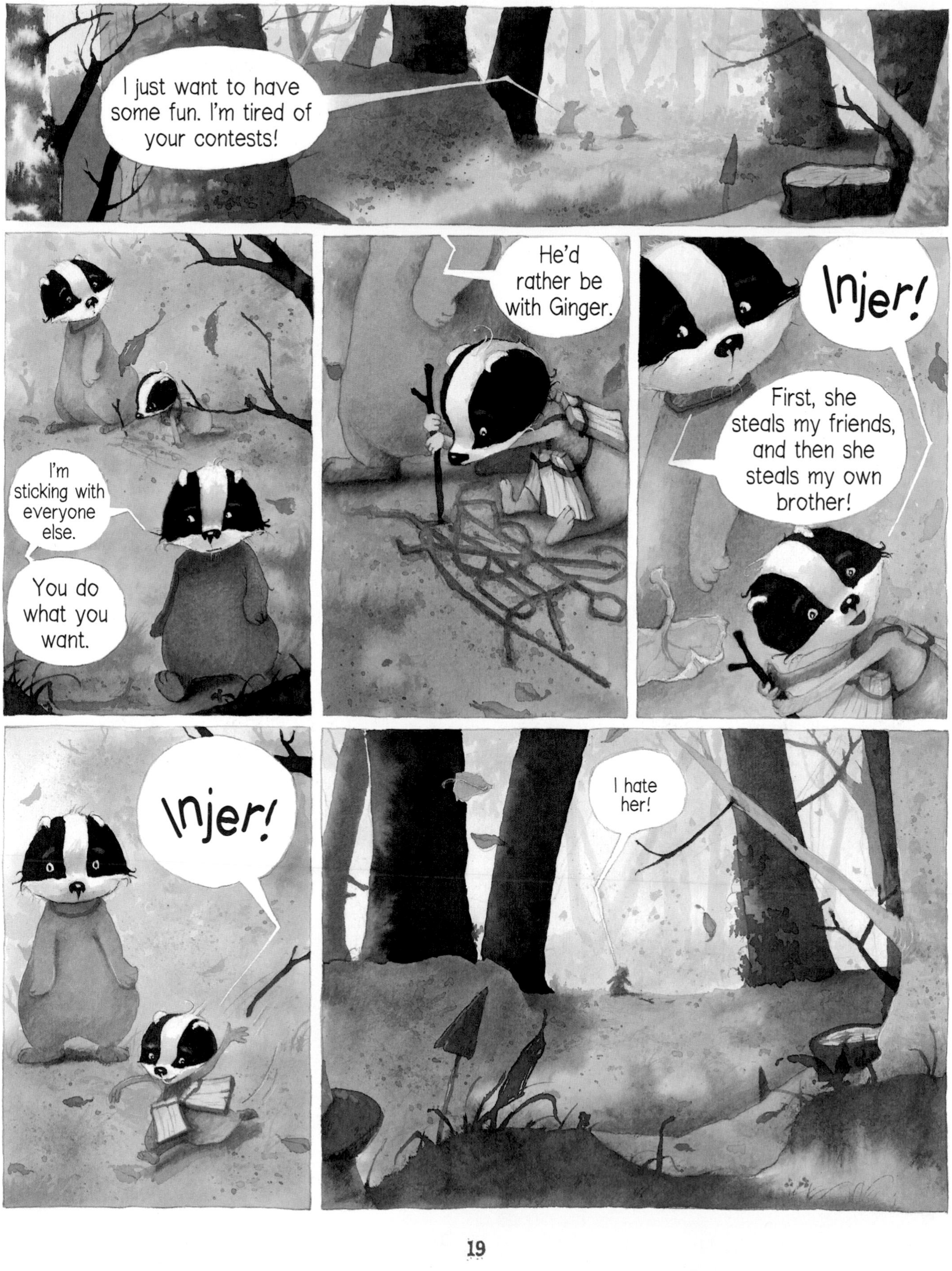

I just want to have some fun. I'm tired of your contests!
I'm sticking with everyone else.
You do what you want.
He'd rather be with Ginger.
Injer!
First, she steals my friends, and then she steals my own brother!
Injer!
I hate her!

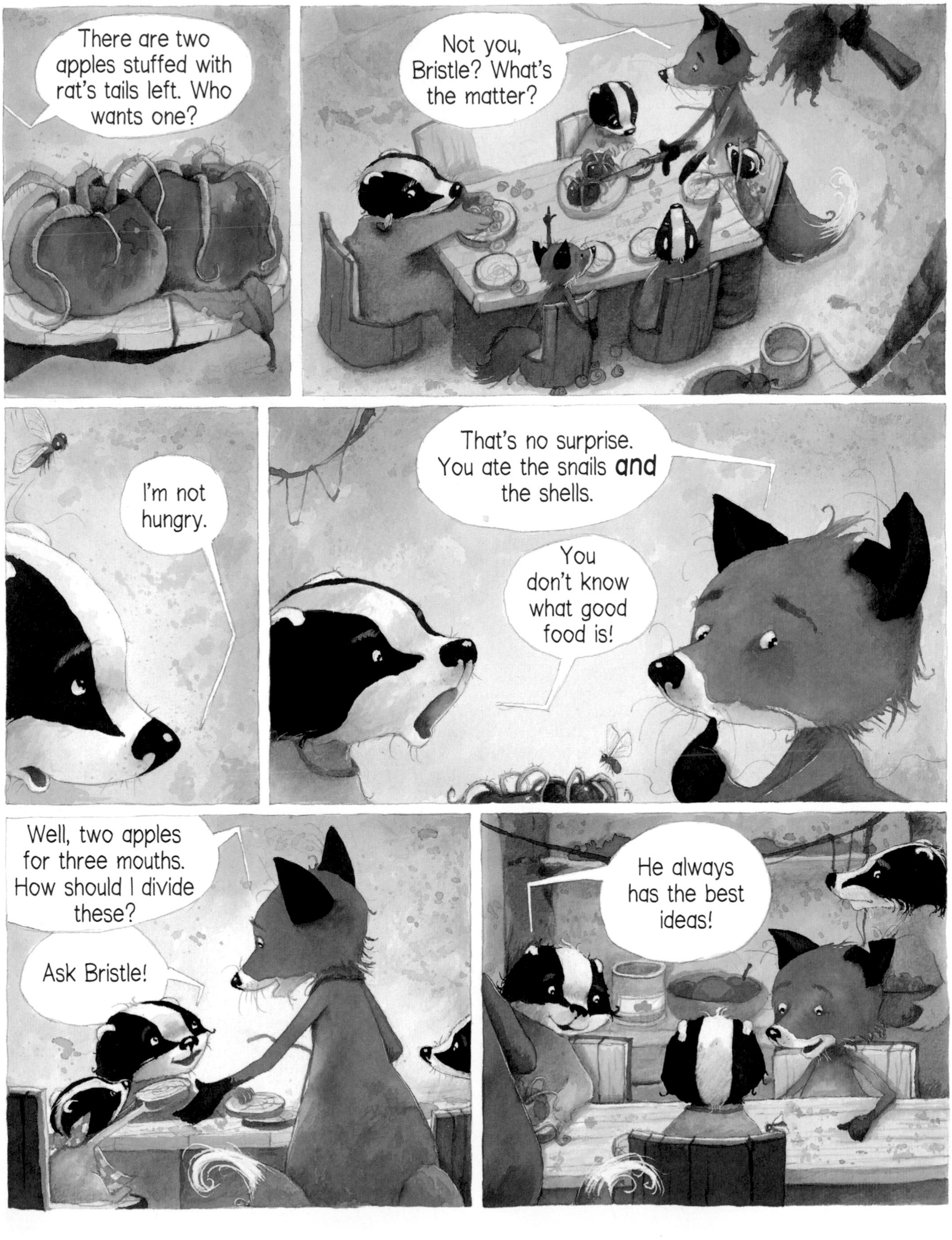
There are two apples stuffed with rat's tails left. Who wants one?
Not you, Bristle? What's the matter?
I'm not hungry.
That's no surprise. You ate the snails **and** the shells.
You don't know what good food is!
Well, two apples for three mouths. How should I divide these?
Ask Bristle!
He always has the best ideas!

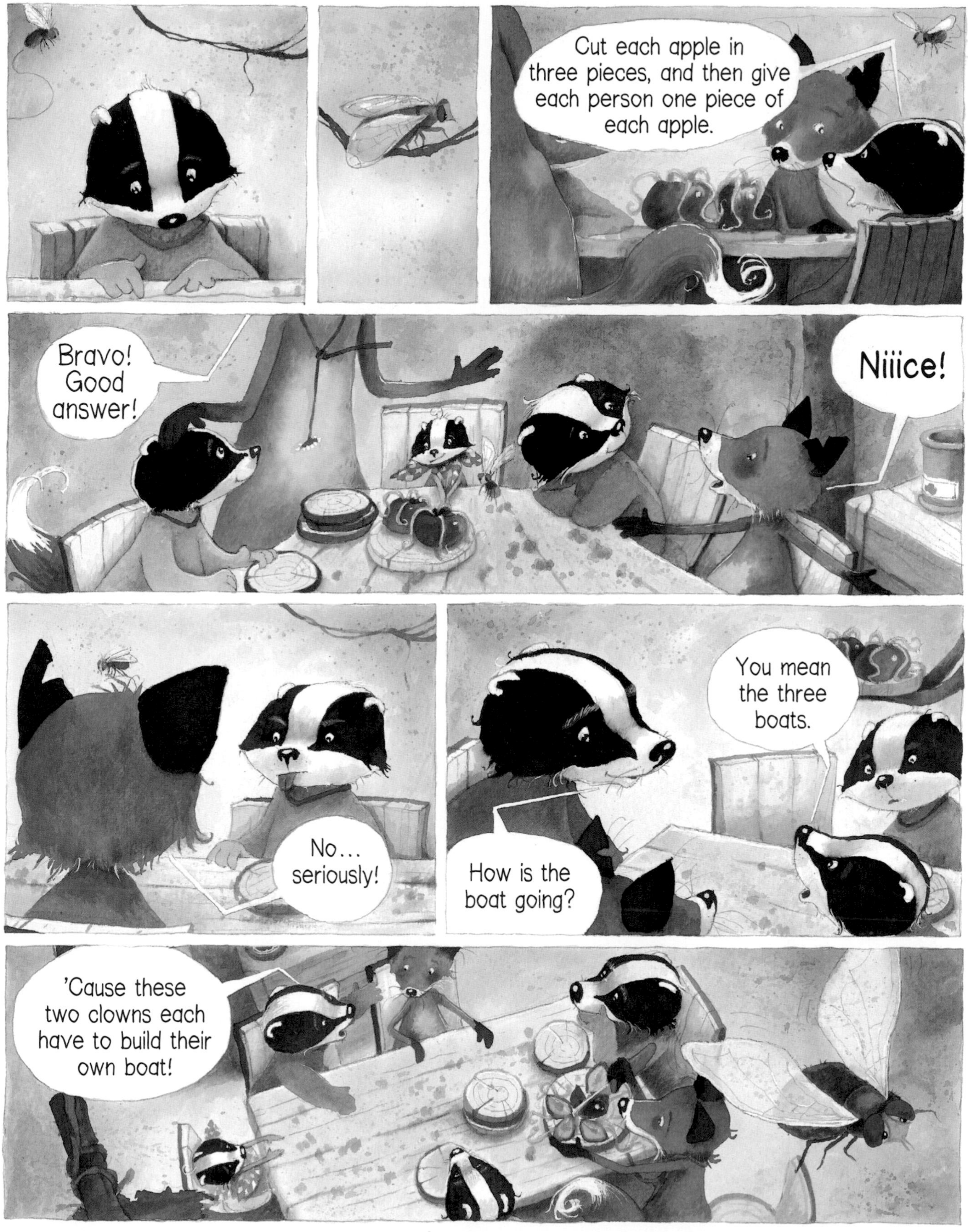
Cut each apple in three pieces, and then give each person one piece of each apple.
Bravo! Good answer!
Niiice!
No... seriously!
How is the boat going?
You mean the three boats.
'Cause these two clowns each have to build their own boat!

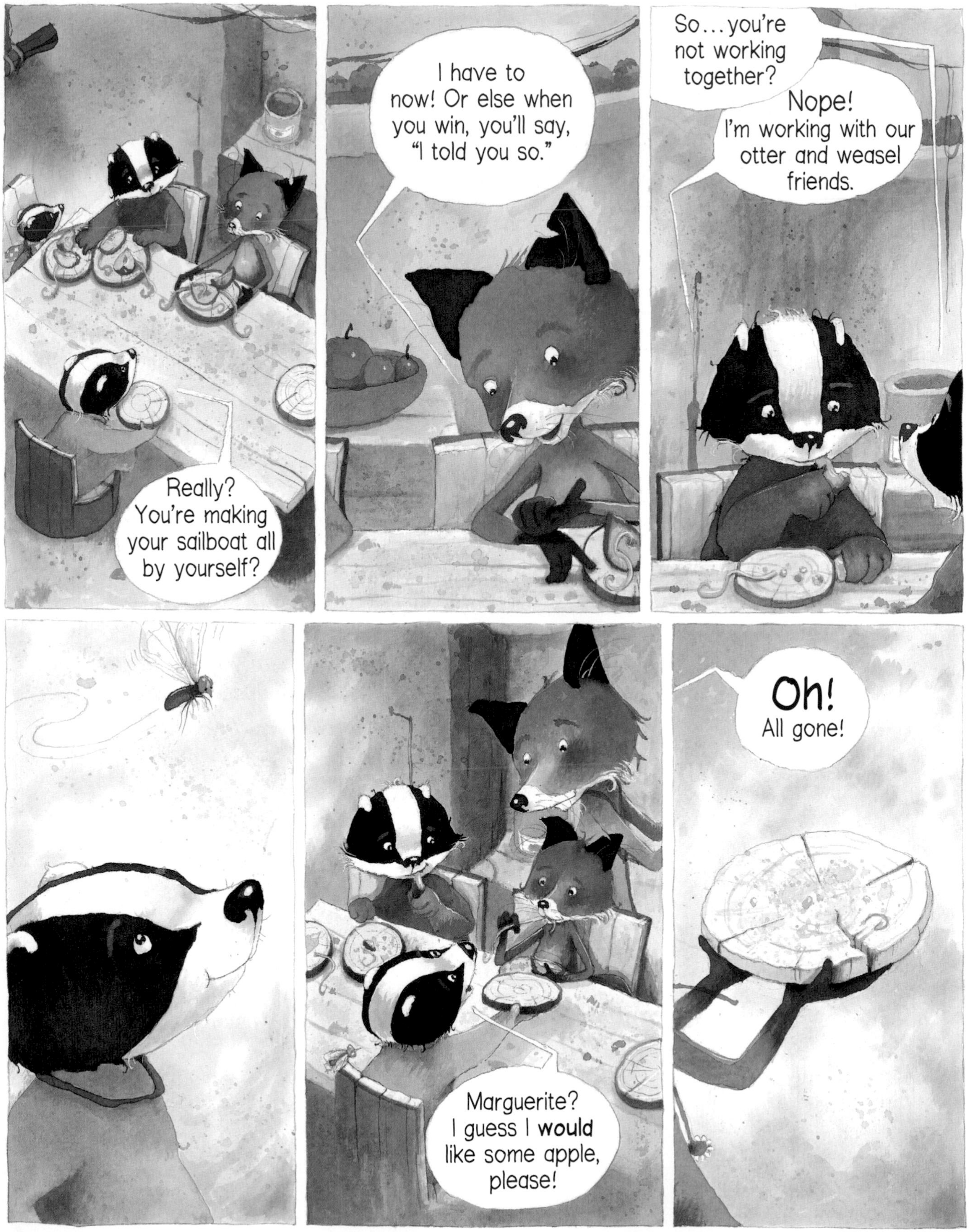

Really? You're making your sailboat all by yourself?
I have to now! Or else when you win, you'll say, "I told you so."
So... you're not working together?
Nope! I'm working with our otter and weasel friends.
Marguerite? I guess I **would** like some apple, please!
Oh! All gone!

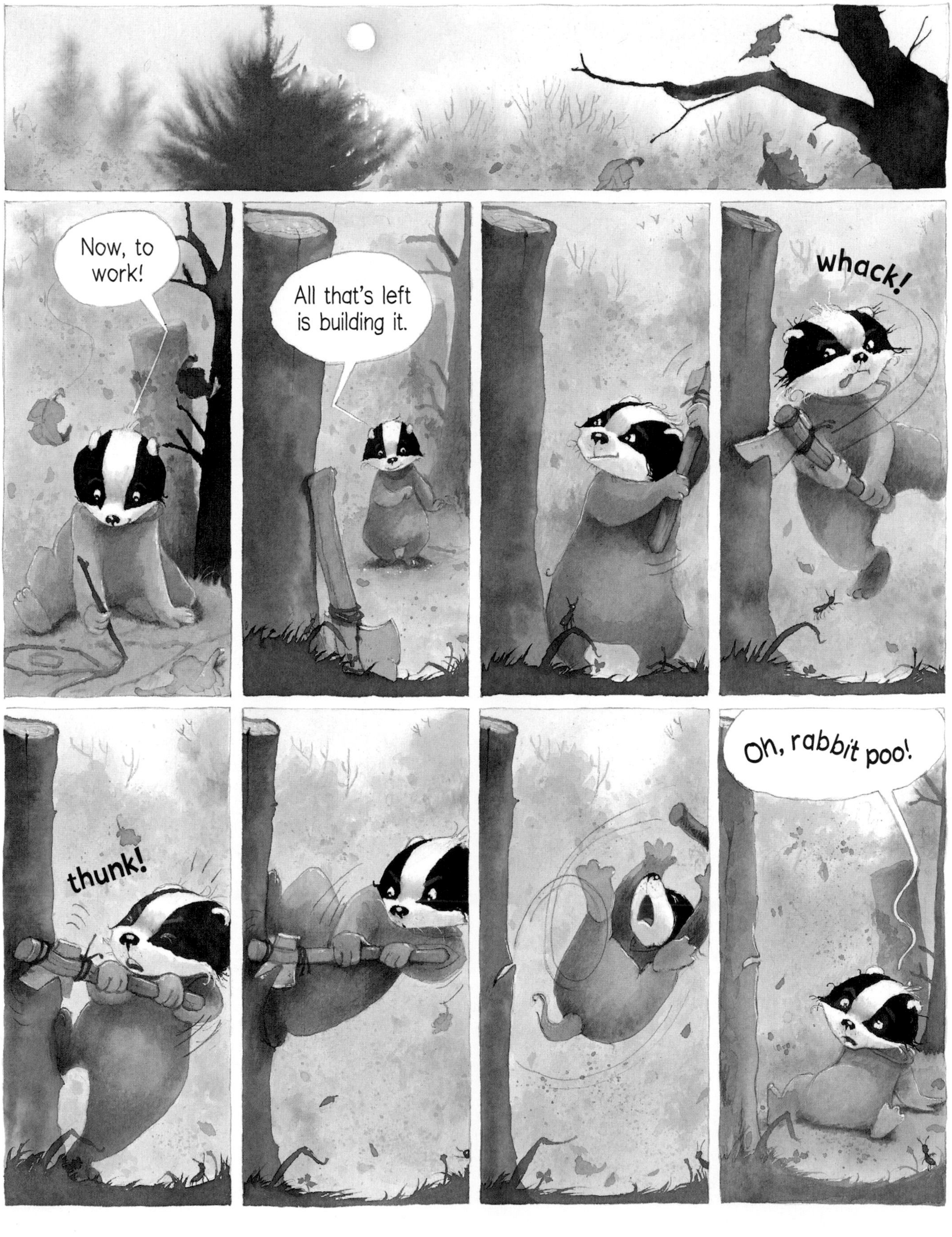
Now, to work!
All that's left is building it.
whack!
thunk!
Oh, rabbit poo!

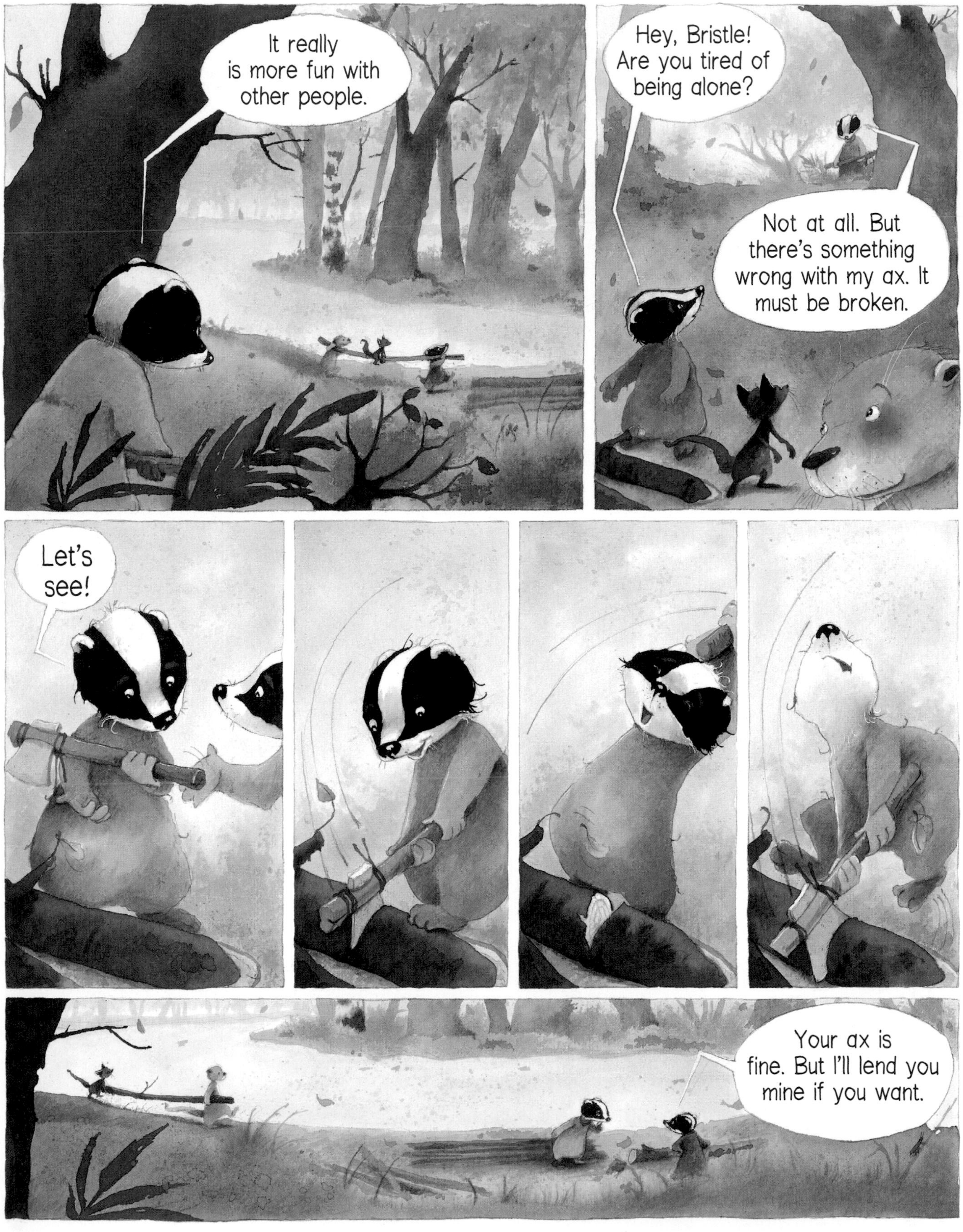

It really is more fun with other people.
Hey, Bristle! Are you tired of being alone?
Not at all. But there's something wrong with my ax. It must be broken.
Let's see!
Your ax is fine. But I'll lend you mine if you want.

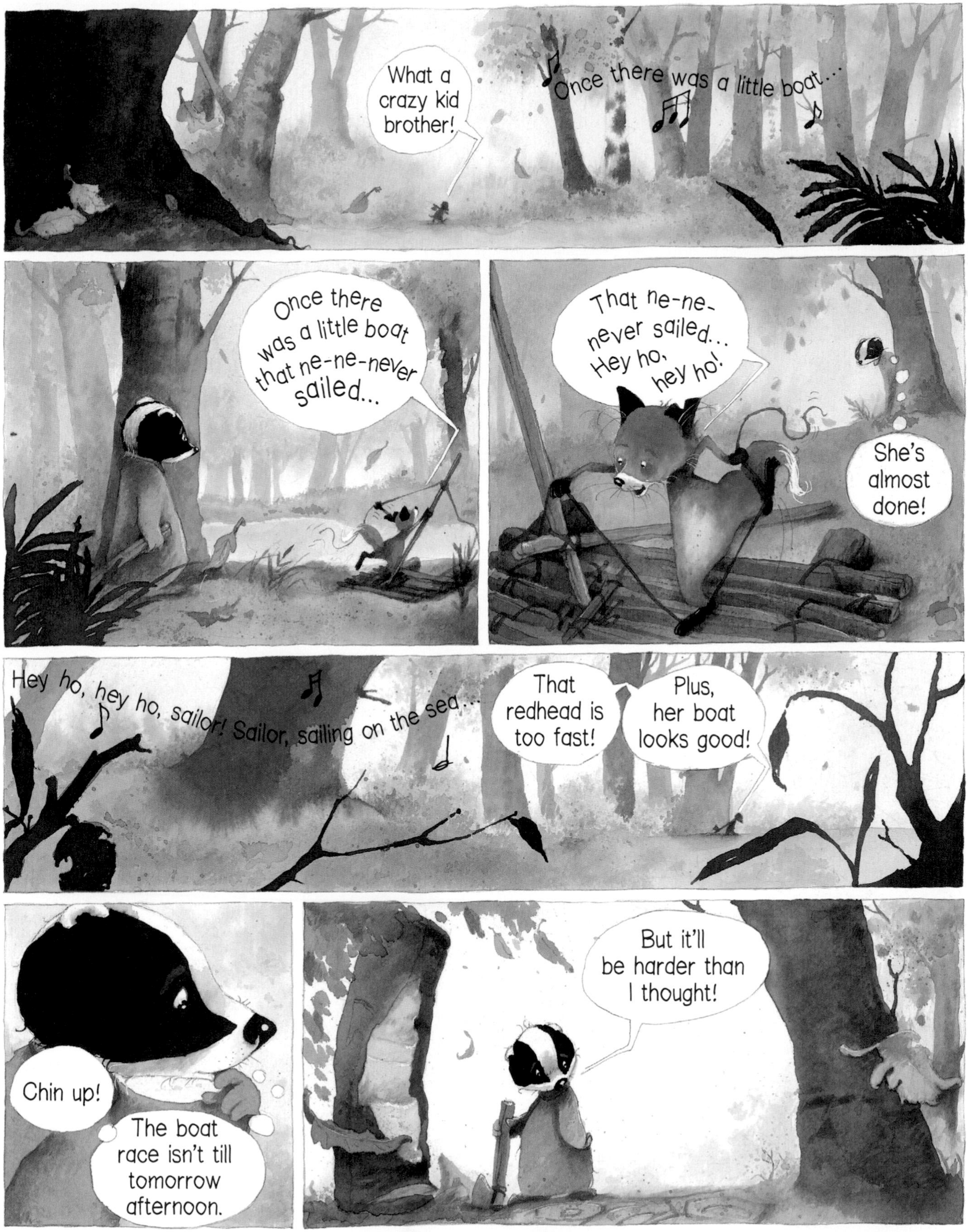
What a crazy kid brother!
Once there was a little boat...
Once there was a little boat that ne-ne-never sailed...
That ne-ne-never sailed... Hey ho, hey ho!
She's almost done!
Hey ho, hey ho, sailor! Sailor, sailing on the sea...
That redhead is too fast!
Plus, her boat looks good!
Chin up!
The boat race isn't till tomorrow afternoon.
But it'll be harder than I thought!

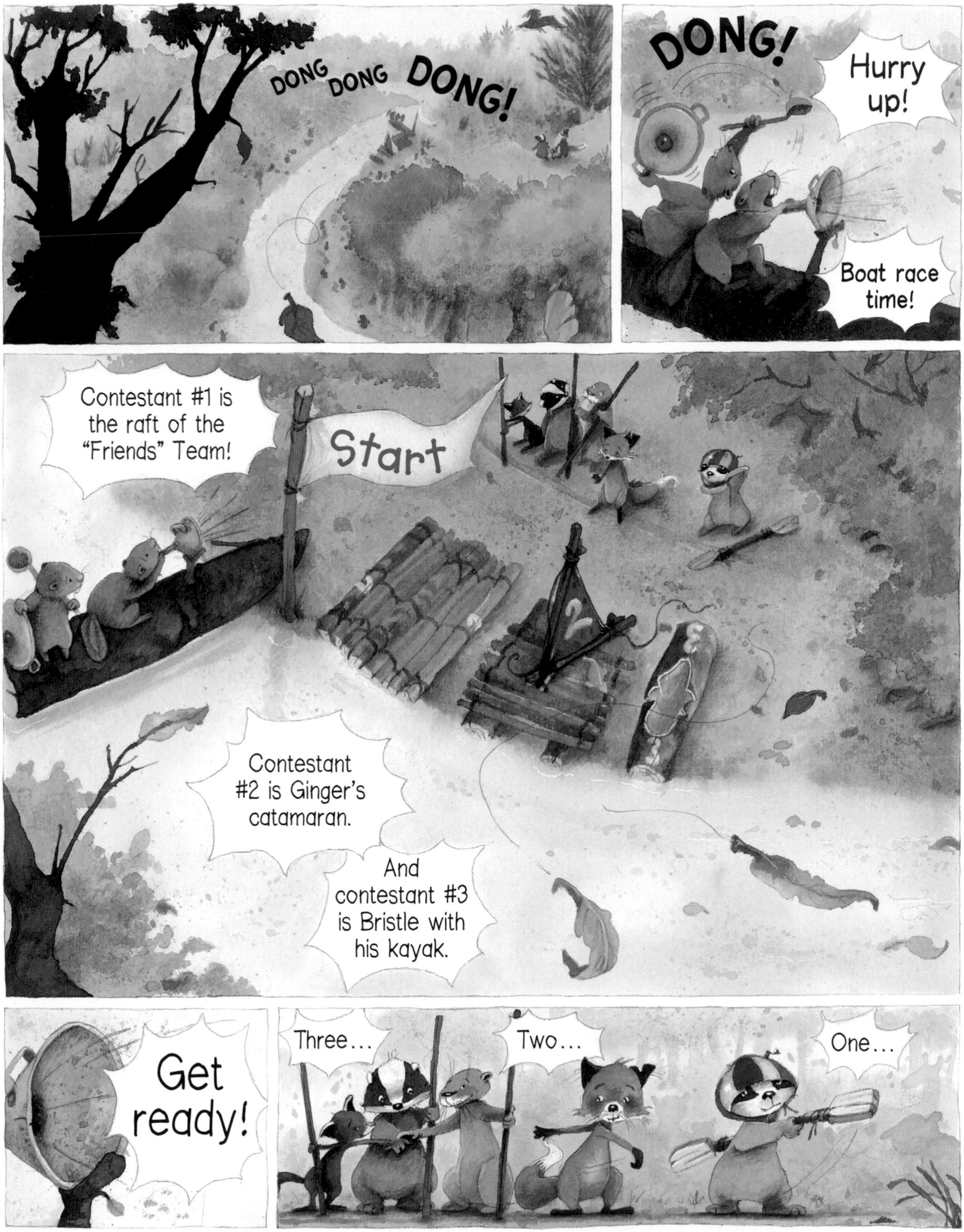
DONG DONG DONG!
DONG!
Hurry up!
Boat race time!
Contestant #1 is the raft of the "Friends" Team!
Start
Contestant #2 is Ginger's catamaran.
And contestant #3 is Bristle with his kayak.
Get ready!
Three...
Two...
One...

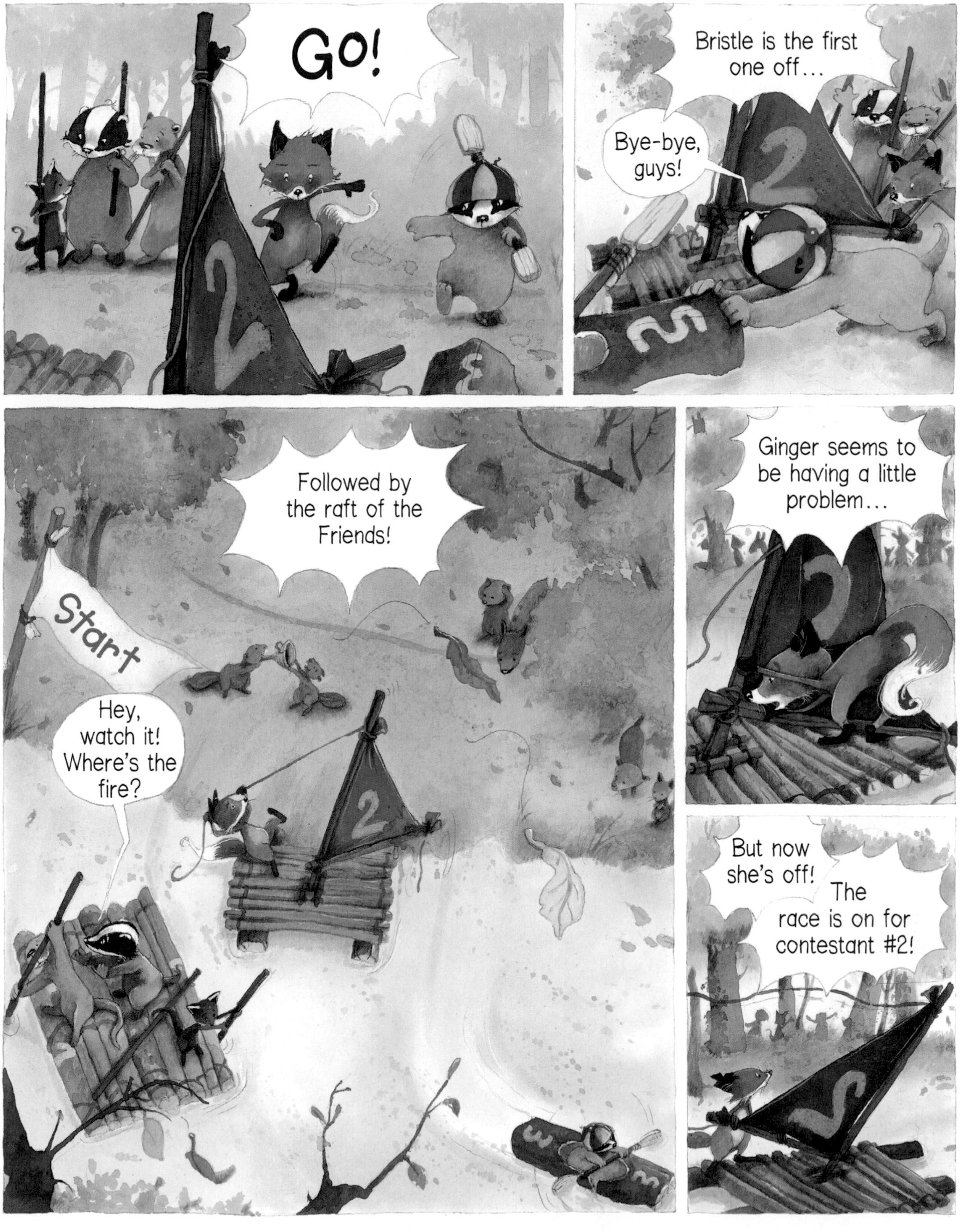
GO!
Bristle is the first one off...
Bye-bye, guys!
Followed by the raft of the Friends!
Hey, watch it! Where's the fire?
Start
Ginger seems to be having a little problem...
But now she's off!
The race is on for contestant #2!

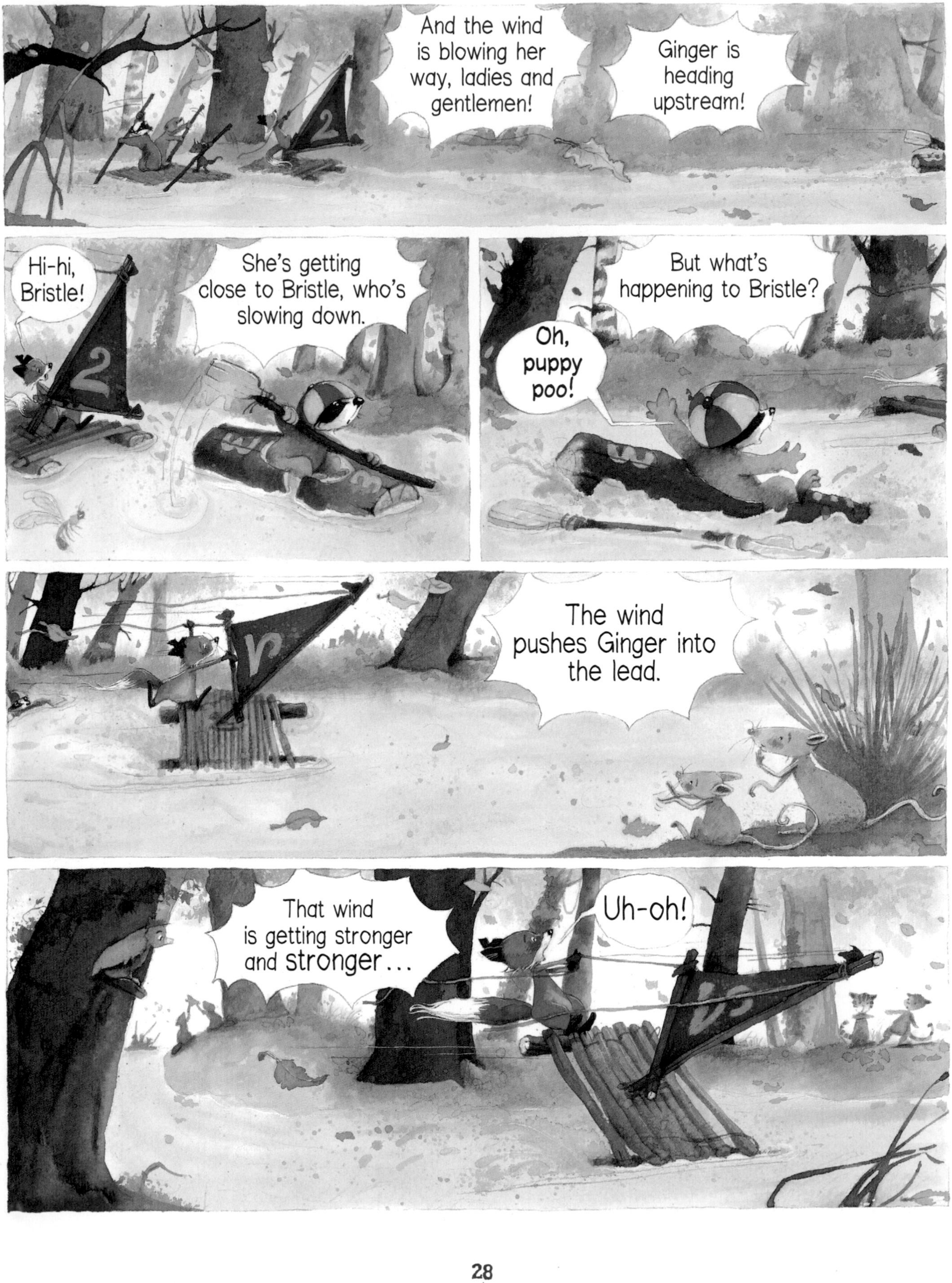

And the wind is blowing her way, ladies and gentlemen!
Ginger is heading upstream!
Hi-hi, Bristle!
She's getting close to Bristle, who's slowing down.
But what's happening to Bristle?
Oh, puppy poo!
The wind pushes Ginger into the lead.
That wind is getting stronger and stronger...
Uh-oh!

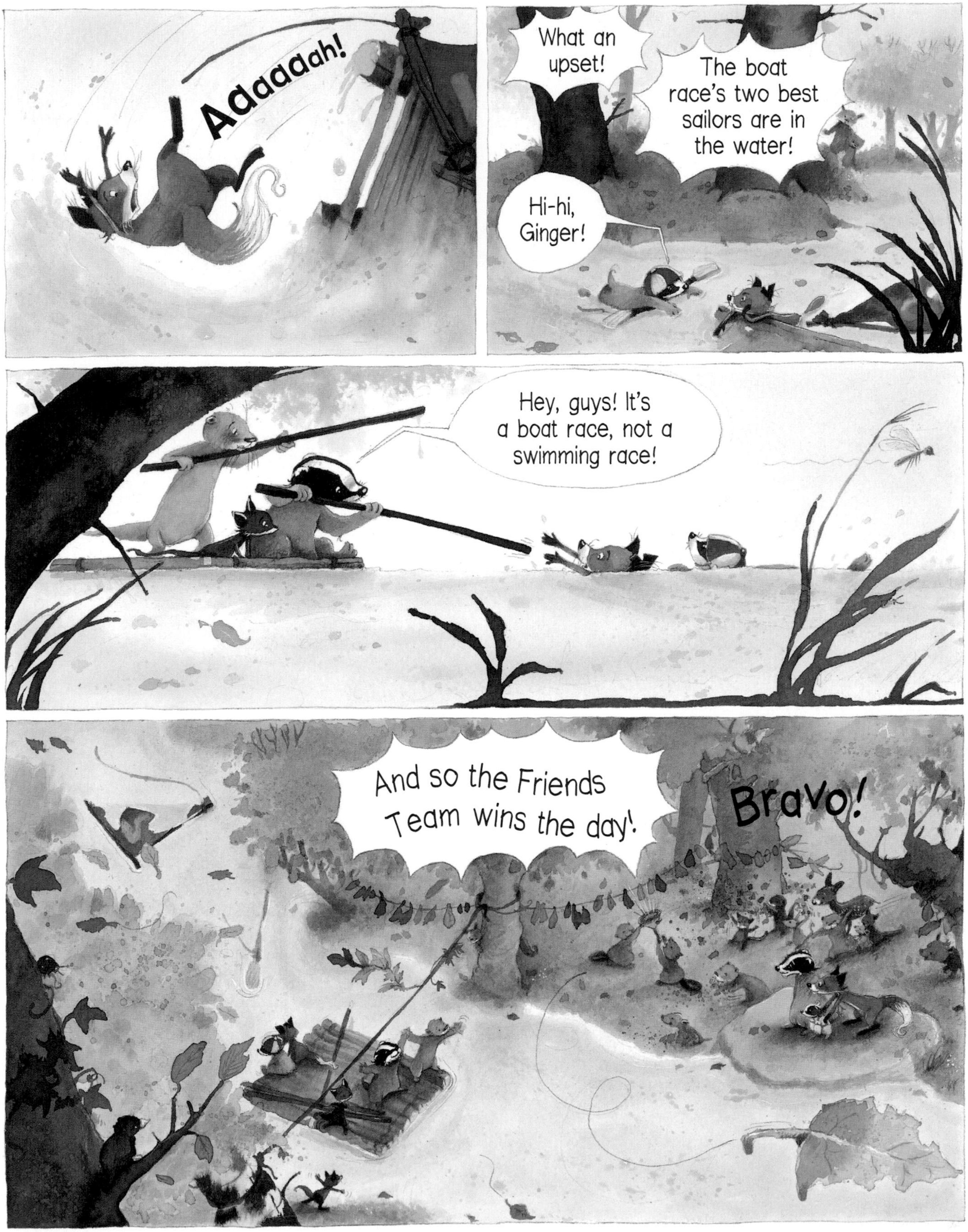
Aaaaaah!
What an upset!
The boat race's two best sailors are in the water!
Hi-hi, Ginger!
Hey, guys! It's a boat race, not a swimming race!
And so the Friends Team wins the day!
Bravo!

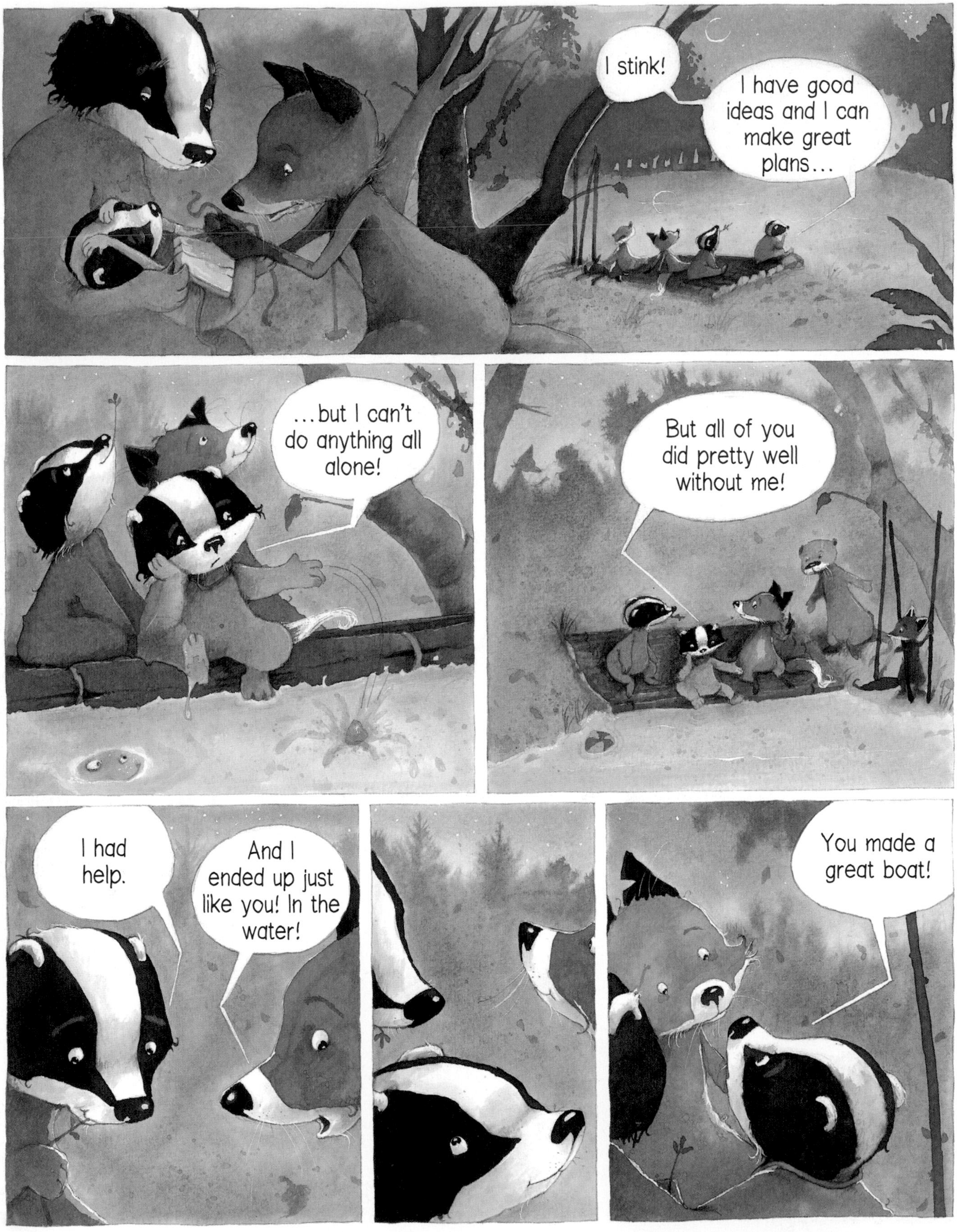
I stink!
I have good ideas and I can make great plans...
...but I can't do anything all alone!
But all of you did pretty well without me!
I had help.
And I ended up just like you! In the water!
You made a great boat!

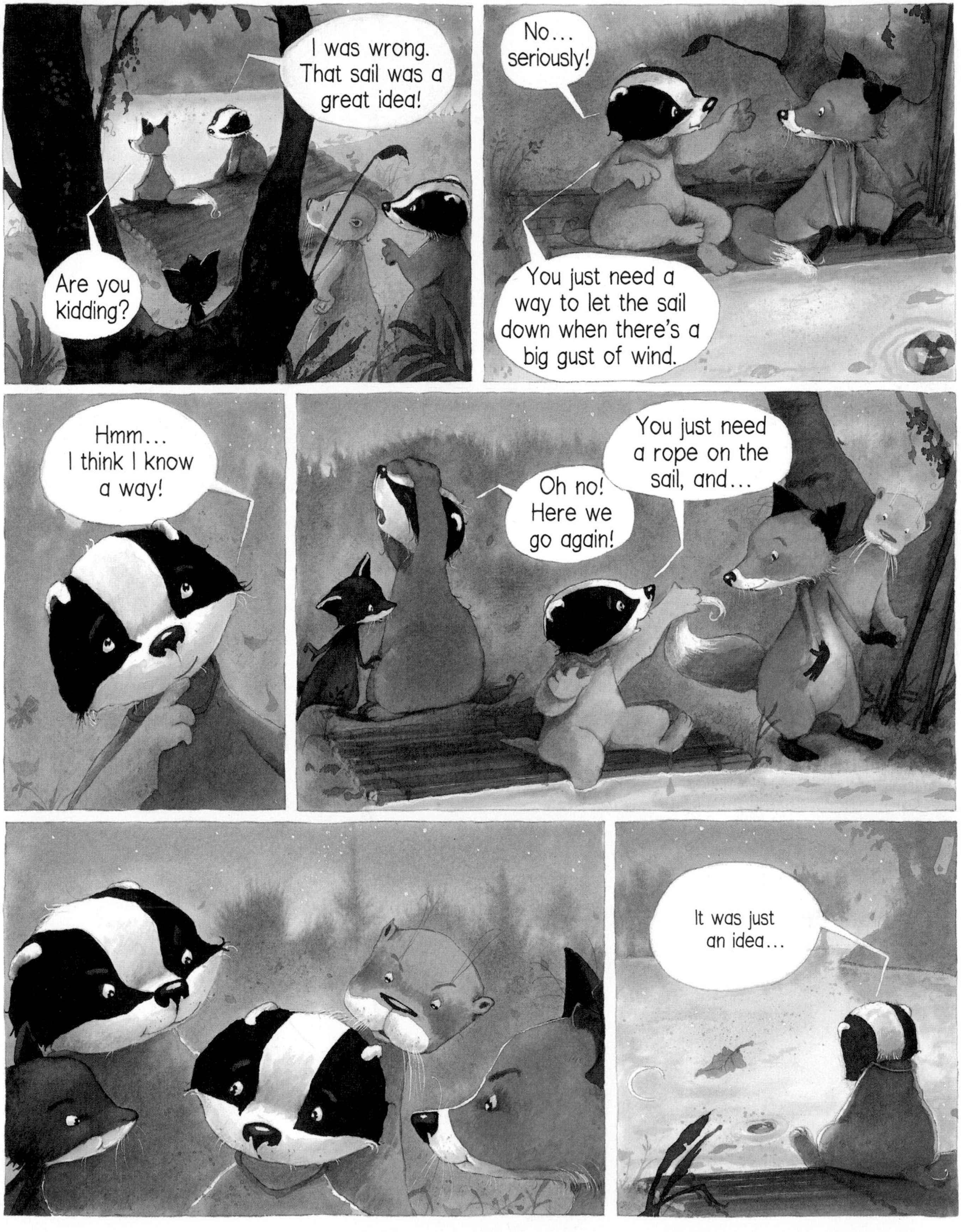
I was wrong. That sail was a great idea!
Are you kidding?
No... seriously!
You just need a way to let the sail down when there's a big gust of wind.
Hmm... I think I know a way!
You just need a rope on the sail, and...
Oh no! Here we go again!
It was just an idea...

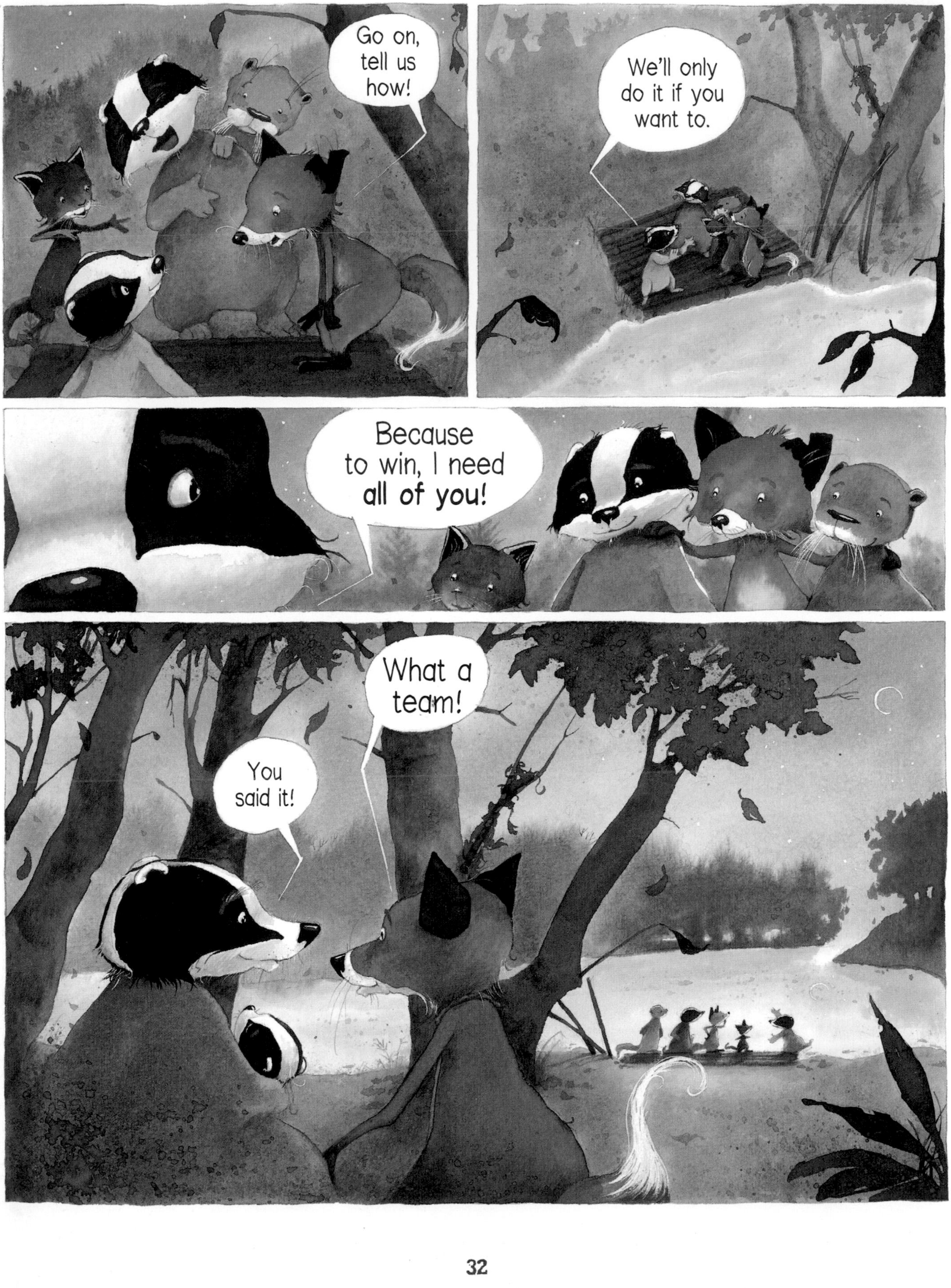

Go on, tell us how!
We'll only do it if you want to.
Because to win, I need **all of you!**
What a team!
You said it!